Lexi

Lexi

L. S. Matthews

DELACORTE PRESS

Published by Delacorte Press
an imprint of Random House Children's Books
a division of Random House, Inc.
New York

Delacorte Press and colophon are registered trademarks of
Random House, Inc.

Visit us on the Web! www.randomhouse.com/kids

Educators and librarians, for a variety of teaching tools,
visit us at www.randomhouse.com/teachers

Library of Congress Cataloging-in-Publication Data
Matthews, L. S. (Laura S.)
Lexi / by L. S. Matthews. — 1st American ed.
p. cm.
Summary: When twelve-year-old Lexi wakes up in the middle of a
forest with no memory of her name or anything else, she slowly
reconstructs her forgotten life with the help of some shelter
workers, an ex-boxer, and her long-lost grandmother.
ISBN: 978-0-385-73574-2 (hardcover)
ISBN: 978-0-385-90563-3 (Gibraltar lib. bdg.)
ISBN: 978-0-385-73575-9 (pbk.)
[1. Amnesia—Fiction. 2. Orphans—Fiction. 3. Twins—Fiction.
4. Sisters—Fiction. 5. Homeless persons—Fiction.] I. Title.
PZ7.M43367Le 2008
[Fic]—dc22   2007046745

Printed in the United States of America

10 9 8 7 6 5 4 3 2 1

First American Edition

ONE
Being Born

Do you remember being born?

Of course you don't. That's a silly question, you'll say. No one asks that. But someone might have asked you: "What's your earliest memory?" Some people remember things from when they were two or three years old. Maybe that's why we don't remember being born—because we were too young, just a tiny new baby, to remember anything that early.

But what if you were born, at say, seven, ten or eleven years old, fully formed?

That's what happened to me.

Of course, I found out later this was really the *second* time I was born. But I didn't know that at the time. So I'll just tell you how it seemed to me then.

It felt a bit like waking up, but not quite the same.

First, there was nothing but a sound. A bird was

singing, a waterfall of notes. Then it seemed to get closer, to be more insistent. The voice of little chimes trickled over my ears again and again, got into my head and started to bother me.

I became aware that I was cold, and I couldn't see. My hands moved, the fists clenched by themselves. Something crunched soggily between my fingers. I was uncomfortable. I didn't want to wake up, to *be*, but my body seemed to complain that I must. Wake up. Open the eyes. My lids were heavy and sticky, but finally they lifted.

A dark blur against a fuzzy soft blue light slowly turned into tree branches with sky behind. I turned my head to one side. Pale golden sunlight flickered along a denim sleeve stretching away: my arm. At the end of it, my hand held damp brown leaves.

The scent of sodden wood and earth rose up, filling my nose and mouth; a mushroomy sort of smell so strong I could taste it.

Slowly I tried to take it all in. I was lying on my back on the ground. I was in a wood or forest. I didn't want to stay like that because bits of me hurt and I was cold.

I found the other ends of my body—my feet and legs; they moved a bit when I tried. I pulled my arms to my sides and bent them at the elbows and pushed myself up from the waist so I was sitting up.

Ugh!

Everything went blurry again, I remember, and I felt very bad, and just managed to lean over and away before I was sick.

I sat there a bit longer with my eyes closed until I felt better. Then I looked around again, carefully and slowly.

This time, things were clearer. I saw trees around me and grass shoots and plant stalks springing up among the brown of old pine needles and dead leaves on the ground. I had a little think. I watched a wood louse mountaineering slowly and determinedly over the leg of my jeans. I stared for quite a while. The soft rays of sun bounced on the curved tops of his little gray sections, making them pearly and see-through. The movement of his tiny legs rolled in a wave along his sides. Two fine-hair feelers waved questions from time to time as he struggled over unfamiliar fabric hills.

3

I checked what I DID know.

I knew I was a girl; I was wearing denim jeans and a jacket, boots and a T-shirt, which seemed familiar enough. You will know by now that I couldn't have just been born, even if it were possible, at about twelve years old. I knew what trees and leaves and wood lice and clothes were, for a start, and new babies don't really know these things, let alone the names for them.

But there was nothing else—nothing else I knew. When I tried to understand what I was doing there—went to the place we have in our heads marked "What has just happened" or even "What has ever happened"—there was just nothing. Nothing there.

So I knew one more thing—that something was missing.

That feeling, added to the general uncomfortableness of it all, nagged me to get to my feet, to get moving.

My head hurt in a big, thumping-behind-the-eyes kind of way, and I staggered a bit as I took those first steps. There didn't seem to be a particular path, just grass and trees. Then, when I was wondering which way to go, the birdsong came again, quite near. I looked up and eventually I saw him. For all his pretty sound, he was a dull little thing of that color between brown and gray, with a slightly paler chest. He looked at me with his head on one side from a low branch, twittered a couple of times and fluttered away. You'll probably think I was a bit silly, but without any better ideas—or any ideas at all, if I'm honest—I plodded after him.

I don't know how long I walked for. I admit I find this part of my journey hard to remember. At points, the ground was boggy and squelchy. I tripped over tussocks of grass a few times, because I was looking up for the bird, and once I nearly walked straight into a branch because I was looking down at the tussocks.

As I went along, though, I found I knew more things. One: I needed the bathroom. Two: I was thirsty. Number three happened when I couldn't see the bird for a while, and he wasn't singing. I got a bit scared, in the middle of the skeleton trees with the sky darkening between their tight, scratchy twigs. So I tried to call to him. I thought I'd make a bird noise by blowing between my lips. Only air rushed out without sound. I put my tongue behind my teeth and managed to make a weak hissing noise. Apparently, I couldn't whistle. And then I tried calling: "Birdeeee?" My voice came out like something old and rusty, but I tried again: "Hey, Tweety-pie!" That worked. Voice came out nice and clear. So number three, I also knew how to talk, though as soon as I had, I wondered why I'd called the bird that name. Couldn't remember. It didn't matter anyway. There he was again, singing to the right, and I was happy to keep following.

Tweety-pie wasn't frightened enough, perhaps, to make the effort to fly far away. He kept waiting till I'd caught up and then he'd do a low dart, a few flaps and a glide, on to his next chosen perch.

Besides stopping once to deal with the needing-the-bathroom-thing, which added to my knowledge collection—that is, I didn't reckon I'd done that very often before out in the wild, and I was hoping I wouldn't have to again—plus a pause for a drink from a tiny stream (tasted good, but I didn't seem very good at that either, as I got very wet sleeves), I tramped on again for what seemed like hours. I'd warmed up in the sun, having got off the cold ground, but as the darkness fell I started to shiver.

The trees changed to a mixture of tall ones and lower, bushier ones with thick, dark leaves. There were fewer leaves on the ground, and more ferny fronds sprouting everywhere. The air grew damp and sticky. Once, I thought I saw some kind of animal out of the corner of my eye, slinking away; at other times, I caught a glimpse of something which might have been a large, silent, grayish bird and the fan of a wingbeat, but I was never quite quick enough to see properly.

Sometimes, between bushes and trees, I saw a silver flash of water.

As I leaned on a mossy tree to rest, my tired eyes found a small pool glittering a little way between the branches and leaves, and there on the fringed edge was a bird of the most incredible colors. The beak caught my eye first—a scarlet blob with a yellow tip, against the dark plant life. Its head and chest were sky blue and sapphire softening to deep, metallic purple further down; its wings and tail were burnished green yet turned dark bronze as it moved; the legs were long yellow sticks.

In front of my eyes, this jewel of a bird seemed to walk silently across the water and disappear. How could this be so? I shook my head, looked again, but it had gone. I turned back to my trudging and wished I could step as lightly and effortlessly as that bird. If it was real.

Then, quite suddenly, because I hadn't been looking ahead, the trees just stopped and I found myself on the edge of the forest. There, down below a rough bit of wild, blue-shadowed ground, you could see the lights of houses, a lot of houses, and other buildings, tall ones, in the distance. Above me was a midnight-blue and starry sky, but above the city a hanging, yellowish glow pushed it back like a pair of dark curtains.

I hadn't known what I was looking for but this

seemed to be right, judging by the relief washing all over me. I turned to the bird, but he was already off and away, flying far back into the dark woods behind me.

Hoping I would know where to go when I got there, if you know what I mean, I set off down toward the first lights.

TWO
Over the Blue Bridge

I had thought that the houses and so on were quite near, but I found myself on a road, walking, and every time I looked at the city lights, they seemed as far away as ever. I don't know how long I carried on walking. From time to time my head felt all fuzzy and I thought maybe I was in a dream and I would never wake up from it.

Every so often I would find myself getting up from the ground at the edge of the shining black ribbon which smelt of oil and dirt, though I hadn't remembered sitting down for a rest. I can't say I noticed when I actually entered the streets with houses on them. I just started to realize I was walking alongside homes with neat clipped lawns and driveways and garages. I must have been falling asleep and waking up on my feet.

Now I was where I wanted to be, I didn't quite know what to do. I looked out for someone to ask—ask what? Did I live here? It didn't look familiar. I read street names slowly to myself (another thing I obviously knew—how to read—but sadly I didn't notice at the time and give myself a pat on the back). None of these names rang any bells, and searching my mind for my own street name or house number produced nothing either.

Finally, I saw the shadowed figure of a tall man in a suit, heading toward his car.

My heart thumped.

"Excuse me!" I called.

He made no reply and now his hand was on the car door handle. I walked a little way up the drive, hoping he would hear and see me. I was very tired and aching now, and growing more scared in the darkness.

"Excuse me!" I tried again, a bit louder.

The man paused, looked around in all the wrong directions, then spotted me. Though the security light from the garage only fell on one side of his smooth-shaven face, I spotted an irritated twitch of the mouth.

"What is it?" he asked, eyeing me suspiciously.

"I—um—do I live around here?" I said. I knew even then, in my confusion, that this sounded silly. I wished I'd thought of something better to say.

"*What?*" said the man; his hand gripped the door handle of his car. In a moment he would be off.

I tried again. "I'm sorry, I'm lost. I can't remember where I . . ."

The man let go of the car door handle and took a couple of steps toward me. His boots crunched in the silence. Looking down at them, I saw they were the dull red of dried blood, made of some kind of skin. I dragged my eyes away and back up to his face. He, in turn, seemed to be looking me up and down. He seemed satisfied, in an *I-thought-as-much* kind of way, and turned back to his car.

"Not from here, I don't think. Get on back across the river, I think you'll find your place there," he threw over his shoulder.

"Thanks," I said doubtfully. I didn't like his tone. I started to walk away, then realized I didn't know where the river was or how to cross it. I turned back to ask him, but by then he was in his car and it roared into life, sweeping by me too close. I coughed a bit with the fumes and wiped some grit out of my eyes, then trudged on again, looking for the river.

It didn't take long before I came to a signpost which said "Sweetside" pointing back the way I'd come; the name didn't mean anything to me. The sign pointing in the opposite direction was to Bridge and Old Town. Looking that way I could see a huge, softly arching curve of blue light, which must be the bridge, I thought, and below, surely that was the river, a sliver of occasional dark and light running between high walls. Beyond, massive buildings stretched far into the distance, each dark tower sending out glowing colors—gold, pink, green and blue—to light up the sky. My heart lifted a little and I headed that way. I suppose I hoped everything would look familiar to me when I got there, but I wasn't exactly confident. Wouldn't I remember a river, if I lived near one?

The bridge was much bigger than I'd thought. I began to cross it on the walkway which ran along the side. No one else was on foot, and very few cars and trucks passed me, the boom of their spinning wheels and engines running up through my boots to my teeth.

The blue-tinted lights which had made the bridge seem magical and splendid from a distance didn't hide its concrete shabbiness close up. I stopped and looked down at the river and thought that I could feel the bulge of air beneath the bridge, and the soft weight of water below that, just through the soles of my feet.

The river was very wide, and very different to the narrow sliver of light which had flickered from a distance. The lights bravely shining down from the sides of the bridge hardly made it to the dark surface, mysterious with constant ripples. Floating heavily across it came the oily reek of unseen, rotting weed and gripping black mud.

And then, gazing down at a pale patch of light, I had the strangest feeling that the glow was coming from *beneath* the water, not shining on it from above. As I stared, the glow became stronger. Now areas sorted themselves into a clump of blue, an area of white—something was coming closer to the surface! My eyes strained in my head trying to make sense of it. And there, at last—was that weed swirling or . . . hair? And was that whiteness a pale face, looking up? The rippling blue which followed—a long, flowing dress? Terror choked at my throat and I drew back, afraid to look anymore. I put down my head and started to run, and didn't stop until I reached the other side.

I soon realized that these streets were very different from the ones on the other side of the bridge, at the place called Sweetside. Bits of sooty green grew through the cracks and litter on the sidewalks. Some buildings flung out lights from high up, but others were dark: empty black holes, like sightless eyes, stared out from their towering walls.

Here there were people; but people who scurried with their heads down, or clung to the shadows. One thin figure of a man staggered out of a doorway, talking, shouting, pointing, apparently to someone invisible.

I didn't recognize anything, and felt more

scared than ever. My head started to pound again and I just stood in the road, away from the strange shadowy people on the sidewalks, put my hands over my eyes and started to cry.

It all happened so quickly. There was the roar of an engine, terrifyingly loud and close, a screech of tires, and I felt a tremendous blow knock me sideways.

The next minute I was lying on the ground with a weight pressing down on me. I could hardly breathe. The weight pulled itself away; as I wiped my eyes and gasped, the crying all shocked out of me, a deep voice said:

"Are you all right? Here, little fool, are you all right?"

A rough hand brushed my hair back from my face, fingers gripped my chin and tilted my head upward.

"Look at me. You all right?"

I gazed at the dark, lined face of the man crouching by my side, silhouetted by the street-lamp behind. It made the stubble on his jaw shine in a sort of furry halo. I found his eyes with mine—big, warm, brown friendly eyes—and clung to that look. He asked his question again and I realized I hadn't spoken.

"Yes, yes, I'm all right."

He straightened up a little and groaned. He was quite a big guy, I saw now, with broad shoulders which hadn't stooped yet, despite his age. A few people had gathered, or stopped on their way past. A kind-looking woman who was short and almost perfectly square in shape clucked her tongue with concern.

"This your kid?" she asked the man accusingly.

"No," he answered, in between getting his breath back. "I just saw her there in the road."

She turned to me.

"What were you thinking of, honey, standing in the road like that? That car would've squashed you flat like a fly if it hadn't been for this gentleman here."

I felt a bit odd lying down with people staring at me and talking to me, so I struggled to my feet and dusted myself off. Feeling stupid pushed away the pain, for the time being.

"I didn't see it. I'm sorry. Thank you," I said, looking from the woman to the man.

The big man eyed me carefully.

"Looks like you've been in the wars," he said, gesturing to my face. *He* could talk, I thought. I could see now that his nose had been broken long ago and he was missing a few teeth. But I put my hand up to where his gaze seemed to fall, and felt scratches on my cheek. I winced as my fingers found a bruise on my chin.

"That didn't happen just now," said the square lady, peering closely. "She must've had those before." Then she added sharply to me, "Where are your parents at? What's your name?"

I looked away from her desperately, at the kind man, as if hoping he'd have the answers, then back to her again.

"I—I don't know. I don't remember."

"Where do you live? You remember that?" the man asked gently.

"No."

He looked down at the ground and then at the square lady. They exchanged glances. She hitched up her bag disapprovingly.

"Maybe best not to find them," muttered the lady, "state she's in . . ."

"Just what I was thinking," muttered back the man—adults have no idea about proper whispering. "Some parents don't deserve their kids. I'll take her to the Shelter; that's the best thing."

I stood there feeling like a useless bit of lost property or something, which I suppose I was really. I looked down at my boots to avoid looking anywhere else, and saw that they and the bottoms of my jeans were thick with mud. I looked at the backs of my hands and saw beads of dried blood; I stretched out my fingers and saw dirt under scuffed and broken nails.

After a bit more conversation and goodbye-ing, the squarish lady went on her way, as she had to be back to feed Vernon and the cats.

"Come on, Little Miss No-Name," said the big

man. "I'll take you somewhere they'll feed you and give you a warm bed for the night and you can tell 'em all about it. OK?"

"OK. Thank you," I said, then asked, "Is Vernon her dog, do you think?"

The big man smiled and the many lines and folds had to travel up out of the way of it, and ended up crinkled around his eyes. It was like the sun coming out, even here in the dark night on the cold street.

"I took her to be talking about her husband, but I have no idea. Never met the lady before," he said.

"You haven't met *me* before, have you?" I asked. "I mean, I don't know you, do I?"

"No, I don't believe so. I'm sorry I didn't introduce myself before I crashed on top of you. I am Joe, and you are . . . ?"

I looked at him, surprised.

"I really don't remember," I said. "I'm not just not telling. I wish I *could* remember."

"Hmm," he said, as we walked along. "And what brought you to be standing in the road like that? Do you remember how you got there?"

"Oh, yes," I said. "I walked here over the bridge, the one with the blue lights on it. From a place called Sweetside; it said so on the signpost."

At least I knew something!

"Sweetside, eh?" he answered, looking at me sideways, puzzled. Someone greeted him and he called back—this happened every so often as we walked. People certainly knew him. It would be nice to be known, to find someone who knew me.

"So—do you think maybe you live there?" he asked.

"No, I don't think so. Before that I came out of the forest"—Joe made a little noise of surprise—"and I didn't recognize any houses, and I asked a man I saw. He wasn't very friendly but he thought I must come from over here, so that's where I headed."

"Oh, did he," muttered Joe, but not saying it like a question.

"But I don't recognize any of this either," I added.

"No," agreed Joe in a nice, understanding way, which was odd, as he couldn't possibly understand.

He put his arm around my shoulders and gave me a slight squeeze, which took me right off the ground and reminded me of all my achy bits, but I knew he meant well, and I just about managed to swallow the squeak of pain.

We got to what Joe called the Shelter at last. You know the look of a scruffy dog that's just been washed and brushed? But you can still sort of tell it is a scruffy dog? This tall building had that look about it. You could tell that until recently it had been like one of the boarded-up, dead-eyed places with sooty bricks from an old fire or just traffic. Its window frames were patched up and painted and it had a Big Deal new front door. What I mean by Big Deal is that it had a panel with lots of buttons to press and a thing Joe had to talk into, and what sounded like about nine hundred bolts and locks which had to be drawn and turned before you could get in.

But eventually a soft, round, quite young woman let us in. I thought for a moment that she was surprised to see us, but then I realized she had drawn her eyebrows on like that, so she couldn't help it. Like Joe, she smiled at me, which made me feel a lot better.

We went through to a room with brightly colored plastic chairs in it, and I sat on one and found out how uncomfortable it was and stared at a box of old and rather broken toys which stood in the corner. The lady with the surprised eyebrows took Joe through another door after telling me to "sit tight a moment," which I didn't have a lot of choice about, in that chair.

After a while they came out again and Joe came over to say goodbye. He crouched down to talk to me.

"Sarah here is going to take good care of you until we can find out where you're from. You get some rest now." And he straightened up as if to go.

"We?" I asked. He looked at me, puzzled. "You said, until *we* can find out where I'm from. So— you *are* going to come back?"

Joe looked surprised, and then questioningly at the lady he'd called Sarah.

"You're welcome to, of course." She smiled at him.

A pleased sort of look replaced the surprised one. "Well," he said in his deep, grumbly voice, and cleared his throat. "Well, I can pop by tomorrow, just to see how you're getting along. If you'd like, of course."

"I don't know anyone else," I said, feeling a bit scared again, though Sarah looked nice enough. I realized that didn't exactly sound like a compliment, so I added, "Anyway, you saved my life," and then to Sarah, for good measure, "He saved my life, you know. He jumped and pushed me out of the way of a car. Otherwise I would have been squashed flat. The other lady with the husband or dog called Vernon said so."

Sarah's eyebrows definitely looked even more surprised after this, but she smiled at Joe and me, and said that Joe hadn't told her this, and certainly now he had saved my life he had a duty to keep in touch.

Joe went off looking down at his shuffly shoes, but with his chest sticking out a bit more, and I took Sarah's hand and followed her up some stairs from the main hall.

"It's late now," she said. "Let's sort things out in the morning. Here's a bed for you, in a room all of your own, which we don't normally have, but you're lucky tonight." And she opened the door to a tiny yellow room with a little window and a narrow bed just about filling it.

"Hold on," she said, looking at me. "Do you remember when you last ate or drank?"

I thought hard, but as usual nothing was there.

"Don't know, but I am hungry and a bit thirsty. I drank a bit from a stream in the forest . . . but there was nothing to eat."

"I'll bring you something up from the kitchens," she said, then added, "If you really don't remember who you are, do you mind if I look in your pockets?"

I looked at her, puzzled.

"There might be something—an address, a name, something?" she explained.

"I never thought of that!" I said.

I started pulling at the pockets of my jeans while she dug around in my jacket. But they were all empty. My heart sank back down to my

25

boots. The disappointment must have shown on my face.

"What's this, then?" she said, and pulled gently at something around my neck. It was a fine silver chain, and by squashing my chin into my throat, pulling down the corners of my mouth, and peering cross-eyed down my nose, I could make out a little silver key hanging on it.

"Oh," I said.

"What?" said Sarah kindly. "Do you remember it?"

"I—I do. At least, I just know it's always been there." I felt the little key between my fingers. "But that's not much help, is it?" I asked sadly.

"You never know," said Sarah. "It might be a clue. Now don't worry for tonight. Have a sit-down on the bed and I'll go and see about some food and drink. We wouldn't normally allow it in the rooms, but I think just this once . . . And a pair of pajamas . . ." And she bustled away still talking, apparently to herself.

With nowhere to sit but on the bed, and being so tired, I was nearly asleep by the time Sarah came back with a slightly stale pie of some kind and a drink of hot chocolate. Over one arm hung a pair of old but clean pale-blue pajamas.

I gulped down the food and drink very quickly and changed into the pajamas before curling up gratefully beneath the blue-checked covers on the little bed.

As sleep started to fold over me, I held the key on the chain about my neck and knew, deep inside, that this was something I'd always done. But in another lifetime, another bed somewhere, in another room, in another house. So that was one more thing I knew, to add to the collection.

THREE
I Am Recognized

When I woke up the next morning, I was scared for a moment because I didn't remember where I was. Just as it was all coming back to me, Sarah put her head around the door. She looked surprised to see me still there, I thought; then I remembered that she just drew her eyebrows like that—I would have liked to ask why, but had the feeling I probably shouldn't.

Behind her, trying to look over her shoulder, was an older woman with very short hair. They both tried to come in as I sat up groggily, but first they got a bit stuck in the doorway, because it was too narrow to let both of them in side by side, and then the room was too small for more than one person at a time. After starting off all polite with each other they ended up giggling, and Sarah stood back and let the older lady in.

She peered at me and asked how I was. I told her I felt better than yesterday.

She sat down on the bed.

"I'm Beatrice, by the way. Sarah says you don't remember your name, nor where you live, nor anything?"

I thought for a moment, in case anything had come back. It hadn't.

"That's right," I said.

Sarah made signs at the older lady from the door, mouthing something without sound, and flapping her hands about.

"Yes, I know, I know what you think," said Beatrice with a wave of her hand, and looked back at me thoughtfully. I noticed the patterning of wrinkles around her face and the tiny spirals of gray trying to show on her cropped, dark head.

"I'm not so sure," she added, without explanation.

Then she asked if my head hurt, or if I could remember banging it.

I told her that it didn't hurt so much today, but it had yesterday. I didn't remember banging it or anything after I woke up in the forest, and even when Joe had knocked me out the way of the car

29

I hadn't bumped it, as he'd had his arm around and underneath me when we landed.

Beatrice was very polite. She asked if she could take a look, whatever that meant, so I said yes, and she started to feel all over my head, pushing her fingers gently through my hair.

"Ah!" she said.

"Ouch!" I said.

"What is it?" asked Sarah.

"A bump!" said Beatrice triumphantly. "Right here on the back. Come and feel. And there's a bit of a one on her forehead too."

Sarah took up her invitation to come and feel the bump, which involved Beatrice getting up off the bed and going out before Sarah could get in. Sarah put my hand on it so I could feel it too. It felt a bit like an egg hidden under the surface, and was quite sore.

Beatrice asked from the doorway whether I'd been sick at all, or felt sick now. I told her about throwing up in the forest, but said I felt OK now. Sarah added I'd eaten and drunk last night.

"And that stayed down?" asked Beatrice. I

agreed it had. Then she swapped with Sarah again, which was quite good fun for me to watch, but a bit annoying for them, no doubt, and she played some sort of weird game with me, where she held up her stick-thin finger with its tip all flattened in a worn-down way, and made me follow it with my eyes.

"Hmm," she said.

"What do you think?" asked Sarah.

"I think the poor girl has had a bang or two on the head and that's what has caused the trouble. Concussion. Seems all right now, but we'd better get the doctor to give her a thorough check-over."

"And the memory?" asked Sarah. "Will it come back?"

I hope so, I thought, and looked at Beatrice.

"In time, I'm sure," she said reassuringly, then smiled and added to Sarah, "And she's not putting it on, I tell you. Look at that face! She's as keen to remember everything as we are to find out."

Then she looked serious again.

"But still, we don't yet know *how* she got the bangs on the head. Or ended up in the forest, of all places. So we'd best go slowly and carefully till we know. We'll try the usual agencies, missing persons and so on. But she might not be listed yet." She stared at me thoughtfully. Her brown eyes were small and clever. There was a strange, cloudy blueness patched over them, like the reflections of sky in the dark pools of the forest.

"Now it's *my* memory I'm worrying about," she added unexpectedly, and quite quietly. "I could have sworn I'd seen this child before."

She gazed at me for a bit longer. I broke the silence by asking if I could get up. Beatrice was all for making me stay in bed without moving until the doctor came, but Sarah pointed out how much I seemed to have been through and survived the day before, and I agreed and went on about how much better I felt, so I was allowed to get up and told to come down to eat.

I ate toast, and cereal, which tasted a bit stale, in a small room which had the same newly painted look (this time, an odd shade of blue) as the rest of the place. I sat at a table on my own. There were another three tables: one was empty, one had a boy a bit younger than me, sitting with Beatrice. He was moving the food around while she tried to get him to eat. At the other table sat a girl of about my age with her mother.

The girl wore her bushy golden hair stuffed into a ponytail and looked quiet and shy. Her mother wore clothes which were thin and worn, like herself. She looked around anxiously all the time, and was eating quickly, like she might have to dash off in a moment. The girl lifted her eyes and caught me looking. To my surprise, she beamed a big, friendly smile—her mouth took up at least half of her face, when she did that—and she pulled at her mum's sleeve and whispered something. Her mum darted me a wary glance, but I obviously passed her test, because she said something back to the girl, who got up quick as a flash and came trotting over to my table.

"Hi," I said, trying not to spray toast crumbs.

"Hi, I'm Honey," she answered breathlessly. "I never seen you here before. Nor at the other shelters. Least, I don't think so. You new?"

"I think so," I said, and seeing her puzzled look

added, "I mean, I don't remember being here before, so I suppose I am new."

"TV's on in the other room. Do you want to come watch?" Her golden frizz of hair bobbed impatiently on her head. I'd never met anyone so—well, up-front, I suppose you'd call it. She reminded me of those super-friendly puppies who just rush up to people they've never met before, like they are long-lost friends. It was sort of sweet. So I said, "Yes, I'd love to." And almost before I had the chance to put down my toast crust, she was hopping about and practically pulling me off my chair.

We went into the corridor and then into a dull, beige room which opened off to one side; a small TV was blasting away to a huddle of empty armchairs of all different shapes, ages and colors.

I sat in a big, old, comfortable-looking one while Honey searched for the remote, in a way that reminded me more than ever of a puppy. The newsreader was saying something about a guy who'd died in a car crash, who seemed to be pretty important in the music business, some big rock star. His picture came up on the screen and I gasped.

"What is it?" Honey looked up from her searching.

"Who's that?" I asked.

"That's Ferdy Majik, of course. Everyone knows that. What, is he dead? Aw, that's sad. Wait till I tell my mum. She'll be upset. Are you all right?"

Honey was staring at me with her misty green eyes. She had found the remote, but stood unmoving with it in her hand.

I realized I was locked on the screen with my mouth almost hanging open, while the newsreader had moved on to something else.

I felt the shock running out of my body and being replaced with sadness. Terrible sadness. I gulped and tried hard not to cry. But why? I couldn't really remember the star . ... and yet I had recognized him. Then followed disappointment, as I realized the first person I'd recognized was a celebrity, and not someone I'd actually known at all, and was now dead anyway.

"You must have liked him a heck of a lot. It's OK . . . um . . . what's your name again? You never told me."

"Lexina," called Beatrice's voice from the doorway behind me. "How about Lexina for your name. Sound familiar?"

FOUR
Honey's Story

I turned to face her.

"Is that who I am?" I asked. "Is that my name?"

"I don't know. It's just a guess. Do you remember it?" Beatrice stood quietly by my chair. Honey stared, obviously baffled, but said nothing.

I felt a warm, strange feeling when I thought about the name. It was a bit like when I'd had the first glimpse of the man called Ferdy Majik on the TV.

"Yes, that sounds . . . right. About right. Maybe . . . Lexi." The warm glow grew and went wallop somewhere in my head and my heart at the same time. It was like something hit a target, right slap-bang in the center.

"Lexi! That's it! *That's* what I was called!" I almost shouted. I felt a stupid grin spreading over my face, so big it almost hurt.

"Of *course*!" Beatrice smiled, clapping her

hands. "Lexi for short! That would have been what people called you."

"That's a nice name," Honey put in, then added doubtfully, "Had you . . . *forgotten?*"

Beatrice gave her a hug; you could tell she was in the mood for hugging anyone near. "She bumped her head," she explained, "and it made her forget. But now she's remembering!" And she gave me a big squeeze next, with her collarbones sticking in me because she was bony. But she smelt like ice cream and the hug felt good.

"How—how did you guess?" I asked, when she had stopped crushing me.

"I haven't found you on any missing persons list yet," she explained, "but I kept stopping and thinking; I was *sure* I'd seen you here, or at another shelter where I worked a while ago. Then it came to me when I was helping to peel potatoes, and I wasn't trying to remember at all! Isn't that funny?"

Me and Honey agreed with her. Especially, as Honey kindly pointed out, as I was quite pretty and didn't look at all like a potato.

Beatrice was eager to go on. Her blue-brown eyes were glittering with excitement.

"You were with your grandmother. And I remember her well—only needed a night in the Shelter before moving into a new apartment. Myrtle. I know where she was working—it wasn't that long ago. I bet she's still there, or they will know where she's gone!"

She looked at me again, hoping for something, but this time I just stared back bemused. I didn't remember a grandmother. I didn't remember the name Myrtle.

"Don't worry, Lexi, I'll get on the phone and see if I can find her and get her to come over. It'll all come back. But first, the doc's here to check you over."

I looked at Honey, who was listening patiently, and felt guilty about leaving her. She mistook my look.

"You'll be OK," she said. "I've had *loads* of bashes on the head, and never saw a doctor, and I've always been fine after a while." Beatrice winced.

"Will you be here after that?" I asked her. We hadn't had much chance to talk.

"Try to be," she said, with one of her huge grins. She was pleased I cared.

"Won't take a minute," said Beatrice. "Just best to be on the safe side."

She came with me up to the little yellow room where I'd spent the night, and stayed hovering in the doorway while the lady doctor checked every bit of me far too thoroughly for my liking—but they explained you can never tell if you might be hurt somewhere and not notice or realize because of the bang on the head. The doctor—a tiny, quiet young lady—pronounced I was fine, the memory loss was a bit worrying, of course (mostly for me, I thought), and to see if anything came back over the next few days, which it probably would.

Beatrice looked cheerful.

"Why yes, already she's remembered her name. Well, when I reminded her. I thought I recognized her, you see."

"There, you're on the mend already," said the doctor. "Anything else?"

I told her I'd recognized the man on television, but then, he was famous.

"Yes, but that's something remembered from *before* your bump on the head. You see! Tell me, do you remember your favorite Majik song?" I thought, then shook my head sadly. She turned to Beatrice. "Find some of his music, if you can. If she remembers it when she hears it, sometimes it brings back other memories—maybe the first time she heard it, for instance—who was there, what was happening, a party . . ." She smiled at me, a kind smile, and held my hand and gave it a squeeze.

"What a good idea," said Beatrice. "Songs bring back memories to everyone, don't they? I'll see what I can do. Can't be hard. Man sold so many records, everyone must have one. 'Cept me, because I'm a little old for that type of thing." And she chuckled. Then she looked serious again. "Any idea how this young lady got into this scrape?"

The doctor was holding my hand still, and looking at my fingers in a vague sort of way. "Well, there is just one thing. You see . . . ?" And she held my hand out toward Beatrice and pointed at the tips of my fingers.

I told you about my nails and the dirt already. I was a bit embarrassed.

"I know, they're horrible, aren't they?" I said, trying to curl up the fingers so they wouldn't stare. "I tried to get the dirt out when I washed, but they are too sore."

Beatrice shook her head, puzzled, and looked at the doctor, who didn't seem to know what she was driving at either.

"I think maybe Lexi has been in an accident. Been thrown, dragged at speed—the nails, you see, are sanded down and the fingertips are sore. But not a road, I wouldn't say. Would've been more damage. The dirt is earth and a little dried blood."

"Ouch!" I said, as she gently dug at my nails with a little silver tool. She stopped trying.

"Looks like an earth track. All I can think of is a bike or a horse?" And she looked doubtfully at me.

"I—I don't think a horse is possible," I said, thinking hard. "I think I'd remember if I could ride. I do know—I do know I can ride a bike. I'm sure of it. But I don't actually *remember* riding one, like, the other day. Or any bike in particular." Then an image flashed into my mind—a much-loved toy, pink and purple, with ribbons from the handles, the feeling of pride. "I *do* remember one," I corrected, "but it's a little girl's bike. It was mine, I'm sure. I loved it. With training wheels. I can see it. But it must have been from years ago."

"Well, I can't imagine what a local girl was doing to end up in the forest, riding a bike," said Beatrice, shaking her head. "No one would want to do that. It's miles away and dangerous . . . I hope Myrtle's all right. The grandmother," she explained to the doctor. "Maybe she'll fill the blanks in the story when I get hold of her."

"And then Lexi will start to remember, I'm sure," added the doctor, patting my arm.

"You go on down to Honey," said Beatrice to me. "And take it easy for a while. Give your brain a rest. It'll all come back in good time, when it

43

wants to. You can't make it happen. Like me with the potatoes!"

The doctor looked a bit puzzled at this, and I took my chance and trotted off down the stairs and back to the TV room.

There was Honey, and now the quiet little boy who wouldn't eat was sitting on the arm of her chair and listening to her intently. I faltered a bit in the doorway.

"Oh, there's Lexi!" said Honey, spotting me. "Come on over. This is Danny."

"Daniel," corrected the boy. His sad, dark eyes peeped out from under a floppy fringe.

"Hi, Daniel," I said carefully, and sat down on the armchair next to them.

"Daniel is a bit upset," confided Honey, "because they won't let him out, and he has to visit his brother's grave."

"Why won't they let him out?" I asked, surprised. "This is a shelter, isn't it, not a prison?"

"On my own," said Daniel quietly. "They would let me out with a grown-up."

"Fair enough, really," said Honey. "It isn't

44

exactly safe for little kids to wander about out there on the streets without an adult. You should know that, Daniel."

"No, it's not safe," agreed Daniel. "But it wasn't that safe when I was out there with my mum. Nor for you, Honey."

"True enough." Honey pulled a face. "I don't suppose I count people like our mums as adults."

I wasn't quite following all this.

"Why—I mean, how wasn't it safe, even with your mums? What happened?" I asked.

Honey gave me a look. "What's your mum like?"

"I—I don't remember. Maybe I don't have one. Beatrice just said a gran."

"Hmm," said Honey. "Well, my mum does her best. But she can't fight a big man. My stepdad beat her up pretty badly one day, and near killed me. So she ran away from home, took me with her. At first we stayed with my gran. But he found us there and threatened to kill the old lady. Then we stayed a night here, a night there, with old friends of hers. But you can't stay too long; it's not polite, and anyway, they don't want my stepdad turning up there, killing everyone and burning the place down."

"Would he do that?" I gasped. "Can't the police stop him?"

"Yes, he'd do that, I reckon. And so does Mum. She used to call the police when they lived together, but it's too hard to get him locked up and while you're waiting for them to do that, he's gonna get you."

"So—so that's why you're here?"

"We ended up sleeping out on the streets, and like Daniel says, you still aren't safe, even with a grown-up, 'cause the grown-up isn't safe anyway. First there are the mad people, then there's gangsters shooting each other, who might just accidentally get you—that's what happened to Daniel's brother, you know. He was a good man, had a job and everything, just walking home from work and *bang*—he was in the wrong place at the wrong time. Then there are the robbers, and it doesn't help that my mum drinks a lot to help her sleep. She sleeps so good then that you can't wake her up to help you *if* anything happens."

"So you stay awake all night and watch," added Daniel gloomily. "Then the next day's just another day with another night coming."

"That's terrible," I said. "You definitely should stay here. It's safe in here."

"Hmm," said Honey. "I wish we would. Or one of the other shelters. That's what Mum used to say. Just till she got a job, got a place of our own. But then she found if she got a job, it would never pay enough money to get even a room. The rents are so high here. And now she drinks more and gets more scared. She thinks he's still following us. She thinks he can get in, even here. So we move on, to a shelter or the streets, every few days."

"But there is someone looking out for us, out there," said Daniel suddenly. "That's what we were just talking about."

"Who? Shelter workers like Sarah and Beatrice? Or Joe, the guy who brought me here?" I asked.

"No, better than just ordinary people. These can't get shot or stabbed or anything," said Daniel earnestly, lowering his voice. I had to lean in close to hear him. Now we all had our heads together.

"Who?" I asked again.

"Angels," whispered Honey.

"Angels?" I squeaked. "Like, in a book—*angels*?"

"Not just any old angels," said Daniel. "These are Warrior Angels. Honey knows. My brother told me about them. All us shelter kids know. And it's why I *have* to visit my brother's grave."

FIVE
Between the Devil and the Deep Blue Sea

Honey got up suddenly, and went to the big window which looked out onto the street. It was a mirror window—that is, you could look out from inside, but people outside couldn't see in, just found their own reflection looking back at them—and it was covered with a wire grid on the outside. She grabbed the beige curtains on either side of it and paused for a moment.

"Storm coming," she said in her calm way. I realized she was right. It was as dark as early evening, but it was only just after midday. The sky above the quiet pavements was turning a strange, dirty green.

"You *have* to know the truth, if you're going to live on the street," said Honey matter-of-factly. "But you mustn't talk to grown-ups about it. They don't like it. They get cross if you do, and pretend it isn't true."

I hoped I wasn't going to have to live on the

street, but I nodded. I wasn't sure what I thought about what I'd heard so far—but I wanted to hear more.

"Go on."

"Did you notice the lights—in the sky, from the buildings?" asked Daniel eagerly.

"Yes, I thought they were beautiful," I said, remembering the view from the forest. "Especially the blue."

He nodded.

"The neon—especially the blue—is like food for the Warrior Angels, an energy source. That's why kids head for it. That's why you headed for it. It's safe there. You won't get attacked if the Angels are around." He paused.

"I haven't seen any angels," I said slowly.

"You can't see them," said Honey, "but they're there all right. But they are having a tough time too, right now." She looked down at her hands. "Sometimes, maybe even they can't be there for every one of us because they are fighting battles."

"Battles?" I asked.

Daniel sighed. "They ruled, totally. Then the

Scarlet Prince—he's, like, the top bad guy of all time—got really powerful and launched a raid on their fortress and they had to scatter and regroup. The Boss—that's the top good guy—hasn't been seen since. My brother reckoned he's just biding his time while the Warrior Angels sort things out.

"Then the Scarlet Prince found he could get into *our* world through doors—portals which used to be guarded by the Warrior Angels, before he drove them out. You gotta watch out for the portals, keep away from them," he added darkly.

Outside, the wind had picked up and started to whine around the building, as if it was trying to find a way in. I shivered. Normally I would have laughed, maybe, at what I was being told. But nothing had been normal since I found myself in the forest, and this place was so strange . . . who knew if these were just stories? And anyway, weren't some stories true?

"How do I know—what does a portal look like?" I asked.

"Old fridges, chucked out. Keep away from them. Mirrors, sometimes glass is enough. And cars, great big ones, or slick, low, smart ones, with blacked-out windows—those too. My brother didn't spot them in time . . ." He trailed off, shook his head and carried on:

"So, the Warrior Angels hang out around the neon and refuel and make their battle plans and so on, mostly at the top of the Insurance Towers at the end of this street. You know the ones?"

"Maybe," I answered, remembering some big buildings with blue and gold light shining from the windows. "How come you know all this?"

Honey took up the story.

"All this happened only in the last year or so. It wasn't on the TV, the news or anything, because the grown-ups who knew were so worried about it, they tried to keep it secret. But we kids knew. All the shelter kids. We had bad dreams. Then some of us, who had relatives who'd died, found they came to us and told us what had happened."

"Like—ghosts?" I asked.

"Spirits, we call them. Maybe, if your mum does turn out to be dead, you'll get a visit from her.

Once a spirit has seen your face, they can always find you again. They pass on the news from the latest battles—let us know what's going on. I didn't have one visit me, but my friend Miranda did; it was her old aunt."

"Oh," I said, and shivered. Honey hadn't quite closed the curtains together; the panes of glass I could still see had gone black as midnight, and the first drops of rain started to smack into them.

"The Scarlet Prince feeds off nasty feelings—hatred, and jealousy and so on—just like the angels feed off the light. He was doing all right in Old Town, but he wanted more. He got pretty cocky recently. Just a few weeks ago, he tried to take on Sweetside as well."

"I walked through Sweetside," I put in, pleased I knew something at last.

"It's where all the rich people live," explained Honey. "The Scarlet Prince got in there through a door under one of the casinos. The people loved him. He was wearing the best designer gear, he looked so cool, with a big car, spending his money.

A couple of staff thought for a moment they saw scales, you know, like on snakes, between the gloves he was wearing and the sleeve of his shirt."

"What did they do?"

"He saw they'd noticed, and he gave them an extra-big tip, a *wad* of money, then they didn't seem to be able to see the scales anymore. Same for other people—he bought them lots of drinks, and they forgot they'd had doubts . . ."

"What happened next?"

Daniel looked over at the door, checking for eavesdroppers.

He leant in closer. "Brilliant. The Warrior Angels got him—swoop!—just like that. Down out of the sky they came as he was heading to his car and they had him rolled up in chains and yelling."

"What did all the people from the casino say? Did they see?" I asked.

"They were shocked. They thought he was a nice guy. The Warrior Angels told them how it really was and said, 'Look, see what happens when we throw him in the river.'"

"Did they throw him in?"

"Oh, yes. My brother told me—my brother's spirit, that is—that when the Scarlet Prince hit the water, it sort of boiled, turned red, and all his fine clothes sort of melted off him, and you could see all the scales, and his hair wet down so the horns showed through, and the bones of everyone who'd ever drowned in the river rose up to the surface." He shuddered.

"Didn't that finish him off?" I asked.

"Though the Warrior Angels had told the good rich people to keep an eye on him, they didn't, and he got away through a portal on the riverbed. Maybe an old refrigerator someone threw in . . ."

The river. What I'd seen there, beneath the water.

"I saw . . . I saw something in the river," I said. "When I stopped and looked into it, on the way here."

Honey and Daniel sucked in their breaths.

"You want to be careful, looking into things which reflect, though I think it's mostly glass and mirrors," whispered Honey urgently. "There's someone even worse than the Scarlet Prince, who uses them to get you."

"The Crying Lady," said Daniel with a nod, "though some people call her other names."

"She wants nothing more than to hurt or kill children," added Honey. "She loves their tears and fear and crying . . . she *lives* off those things!"

I gulped.

"What—what does she look like?"

"No one knows—at least, no one lives to tell," Honey hissed back. "She comes out of mirrors, out of glass, and if you see her, you're dead. People say that they hear the terrible crying and wailing she makes."

"It can't have been her I saw then," I said, "because I didn't hear any wailing and I'm not dead." I pinched my arm to check I was real. "Maybe it was nothing. I thought I saw long hair, and a long blue dress . . ."

"Beneath the water?" exclaimed Honey, forgetting to whisper for a moment. She looked at Daniel; he looked at her.

"The Blue Lady," breathed Daniel.

"Is—is she bad?" I asked, remembering the fear pounding in me as I'd run from the bridge.

"No, no," squeaked Honey, pushing back her blond frizz excitedly. "She's wonderful. She's a mer-angel."

"Lives underwater, in the sea, in the river," added Daniel. "She's a friend to all children. She does her best to protect us all. More powerful than the Crying Lady; even the Scarlet Prince couldn't get past her—except—"

I knew there'd be a catch. "Except what?"

"Since all the trouble began—well, they couldn't defeat her, but she's under a spell," said Honey, "and her true power to save any child from danger can only be freed if you call her. And you have to know her real name to do that."

"So—the Blue Lady isn't her real name? What is?"

"No one seems to know. It's been lost, or hidden," said Honey sadly. "But they do say it might come to you in your hour of need. That's what I hold on to and believe."

"I've forgotten so much, I'm not sure it would come to me," I said.

"Let's hope you never need it," said Honey.

There was a sudden crack of thunder outside and we all jumped. A squall of wind battered hard, steely rain against the glass.

I thought how good it felt not to be out in that. I should have paid more attention to that feeling.

SIX
Daniel's Task

That afternoon, Sarah gave us some books, pens and paper. The books were a bit like schoolbooks crossed with quiz books, with quite easy questions and exercises in them, like little games. Daniel ignored the reading and questions, but copied a few of the pictures. Sarah came and tut-tutted, and tried to get him to do what he was supposed to, but it was difficult for her, even I could see. He was a cute kid, with his golden skin, and sad, spaniel eyes peeking out from beneath his shiny dark fringe, so it was hard to be tough with him. Besides, he was really quite good at drawing, especially for his age.

Me and Honey worked together, and argued in a friendly way about turns with the crayons. I noticed that Daniel, sitting a little way apart from us, kept pausing in his drawing to stare through the window at the storm outside.

I lowered my voice so he wouldn't hear—though

I think he was far off in some other place anyway—and asked Honey why it meant so much to him to visit his dead brother's grave.

"Half brother," she corrected. "That's why he was so much older than Daniel. Daniel's mum had him years ago with her first husband . . . she's gone and disappeared now, either upped and left, or maybe dead somewhere. Daniel woke up on the street under the old bit of plastic sheet they'd pulled over themselves, and she was gone. He came here because he didn't know what else to do. Now he's scared of sleeping, because she disappeared while he slept and he doesn't know what else might happen while he's not awake. He thinks maybe something bad happened to her when he should have been on guard. Though that's silly, I told him, because his mum had told him to sleep."

"It's silly anyway, because he must be about—what—nine years old?" I said crossly. Honey was obviously used to this kind of life, but I certainly didn't seem to be. I went on more calmly, remembering none of Daniel's situation was Honey's fault: "This half brother—Daniel calls him

60

brother, anyway—tell me why this visit matters so much . . ."

"Well," said Honey, "you want your spirit, your loved ones' spirits, to go and live with the Warrior Angels, of course. They live in the forest, so—"

"The forest? But I was there! When I woke up. I didn't see . . . at least I don't remember . . . a bird or two . . ."

"In an *enchanted* part," explained Honey. "I don't think you can just walk there. A spirit certainly can't. Anyway, it's guarded by some kind of fierce creatures. So you lay a special leaf on the body—or the grave—it'll have to be the grave in Daniel's half brother's case, as he's already buried—I expect that'll be all right . . ." She scrabbled in the plastic tray for a particular color she wanted among the crayons. I saw she was in the middle of coloring some hills in her picture.

"Yes, yes, go on," I said impatiently, passing her a green crayon which I realized had been lying under my hand. She sniffed and took it with dignity.

"Anyway, this is like the person's ticket to the

Warrior Angels' patch. Peace and everything you want, probably cherry-cola fountains and ice cream, forever and ever." She colored vigorously.

"And he's got this leaf?" I asked.

"Yup," she said. "An olive leaf, I think. Only tiny. Or you can use a palm leaf. But he didn't get one of those." She paused in her coloring and looked keenly at me. "What was the forest like? I've never been there."

"Well, I don't think I saw the secret bit. No cherry-cola fountains, or I would have found them!" I said truthfully.

Honey laughed.

"I just added that in," she admitted. "My idea of what would be perfect. Go on."

"It *was* really beautiful, now you mention it," I said, remembering. "Every kind of green," and I picked through the green crayons in front of me, "lime, emerald, moss, olive—and water which tasted good. And in a pool, the most beautiful bird I ever saw, all different colors which changed with the light, like a jewel, on long, yellow legs."

Honey was gazing at me, but her eyes, like

Daniel's, were looking into a world far, far away from the beige room.

"Ooh," she said. "It sounds lovely. Just like I imagined. Maybe I will go there one day. If I get the chance. If the Crying Lady doesn't get me first. She gets lots of the kids."

She didn't sound frightened, just matter-of-fact.

"You look after yourself, Honey. She won't get you," I said, carefully shading a bit of the map I was drawing to show the blue sea. I still wasn't sure how much to believe in these stories, though I knew I'd seen something in that river and I was willing to trust people who knew more about this place than I did. "We could ask Sarah if she'd take Daniel to see his brother's grave."

"She's already said she'll take him, but not till tomorrow. Daniel can't explain to her why he wants to go so badly; all the grown-ups say that talk of leaves and spirits and so on is silly or even wicked. Daniel worries about the spirit trapped at the grave, waiting and waiting."

"That's nice of Sarah, anyway," I said, "and he should just take his mind off it."

I called over to him, "Here, Daniel, show us what you've drawn," and he shook himself out of his trance, picked up his book and came over to us.

The rest of that afternoon was a bit dull. I asked Beatrice if Joe might come and see me, and she said she thought he might, but she was pretty sure he worked at least two shifts at his job, so it would be when he could fit it in.

"People have to work hard, to live here," she explained. "I'm having the same problem trying to catch Myrtle, your grandmother. I've found the factory where she works, but they tell me she also works a shift at a warehouse, so I've got to phone there too and try to get a message passed on to her when she shows up."

I didn't say anything, but was surprised that anyone would want to live around here, let alone hold down loads of jobs to afford it.

The evening came in without us hardly noticing the difference from the dark, stormy afternoon. One bright spot was that Sarah put the TV on to a channel which was showing a whole program about Ferdy Majik.

"They'll play some of his records," she said. "And you might remember them. Oh! This is one of my favorites—'Hey Girl'—do you know this one?"

"Shh!" said Honey. "Let her hear it then!"

I stared at the screen. The man I'd recognized— a good, friendly face—was on a big stage with a heck of a suit on, and was striding about as the music started up. I felt my feet start to tap and my body start to sway with the rhythm. It was like a feeling of excitement, which ran up through your feet to your chest. You had to hold your arms out and wiggle your hands to let it out of the fingertips and still the power pushed up from your lungs and pulsed in your throat till it had to be let out with your voice, as a song. You closed your eyes so that you could feel it even more. You had to dance and sing it out of you. And I knew this song and loved it.

Sarah shrieked with joy.

"That girl can dance, no question!"

I opened my eyes as I danced and sang and saw Sarah joining in. Honey was trying to shush her, but soon got caught by the beat and melody and

65

danced, sang and clapped along with us. Even Daniel, though he didn't get up from his chair, smiled and tapped his foot.

Beatrice put her head around the door just as the music faded out and the boring presenter appeared again, interviewing someone who knew the star.

"Are we having a party in here?" she asked. "Why wasn't I invited?" Then she saw what was on the TV and said, "Ah-ha! Ferdy, is it? Poor boy. Well, Lexi, what did you think of when you heard that tune?"

I closed my eyes and hummed gently, to keep the moment going. I remembered—I remembered dancing and singing along in a bedroom, in *my* bedroom, I thought now. Then I was singing along with the song in a car.

I started to tell them this, but I was a bit short on detail. The truth is, I didn't know how much was true and how much was imagination. For one thing, the bedroom seemed to be huge, and white and pink, like a palace. The car was like one you see on the TV, for film stars, not like one you'd actually travel in—longer than normal, and with soft suede seats. Maybe, I thought, things seemed bigger because I was remembering them from when I was small. For a moment, with my eyes closed, I thought I remembered Ferdy Majik himself, up close, talking to me: "Listen to the beat—wait for it—there! Now the strings come in! Isn't that something—I only added that on the final mix and it really makes the whole song. . . ." But of course, when I opened my eyes, there he was, saying that on the TV.

This was going to be the trouble, I realized, with getting my memory back. Some things were real, and had happened. Some things were mixed up with stuff I'd heard and seen on the TV perhaps, or imagined. Maybe it would all be better when I was back with Myrtle. But I pushed her to the back of my mind. I was worried that I didn't have any particular memory of that name, let alone a face to go with it.

We all went to bed early that evening, maybe because of the storm bringing darkness so early. I lay there in the narrow bed, in the little yellow room, listening to the wind hurling rain against the windows in sudden bursts, like volleys of arrows, thinking about Myrtle. I couldn't think about a real person, because I didn't remember her, but I wondered what would happen when we met. What if I didn't recognize her? My own gran? How would that make her feel? Maybe I *would* recognize her, but if not, shouldn't I at least pretend?

The worrying must have merged into dreams, without my realizing I'd fallen asleep. But I must have, because I was suddenly jolted awake. I wasn't sure what had woken me. I blinked a couple of times in the darkness and listened. The wind had quieted a little for the moment but—there! That was the sound which had woken me.

Someone—or something—was scratching at the door.

SEVEN
The Crying Lady Strikes

You know what it's like when you hear something in the night which frightens you—you have a choice: pull the covers over your head and try to go back to sleep, or get out of bed and investigate. As people in scary films *always* make the mistake of getting out of bed (along with making other crazy decisions such as "There's a creepy house, let's go and ask if we can stay there for the night"), I tend to stick with the head-under-the-covers approach.

I was just about to do that when I heard a hissing sound.

"Lexi!"

I hopped out of bed and hit my knee on the opposite wall, hobbled to the door and opened it.

There was Honey, her blond hair picking up a glow from the hall night-light, making a crazy halo in the darkness, her sea-green eyes huge. I was pretty spooked.

"What's the matter?" I whispered.

"What's the matter?" she hissed, at almost the same moment.

"*What?*"

"Have you hurt yourself or something?"

I realized I was speaking through teeth clenched together with pain while rubbing my knee.

I hissed back—it's difficult to whisper when you are quite cross. "*I just banged my knee* getting out of bed for *you!* What are you doing at my door?"

"Shhh!" she whispered, far too loudly in my opinion. "It's Daniel. He's just gone. Out on his own. I'm going after him, I know where he's headed. Are you coming?"

I stared at her as if she was mad.

"Shouldn't you just tell Beatrice or Sarah?"

"I don't think they'll risk going after him. They'll just tell the police. If we hurry, we'll catch him up and get him back without them knowing. They might lock him up otherwise."

"Oh, Honey," I groaned.

"I'll go on my own then," she whispered, and turned to go.

What to do? Go and tell someone and go back to bed? But then Honey would be gone already, and out on her own.

No one's at their best about making sensible decisions when woken in the middle of the night. That's my excuse, looking back.

"Hold on a sec. Let me get my clothes on."

I was dressed in a flash, and creeping down the dark hallway after Honey a moment later.

You know what it's like when you're trying to be quiet—the soles of my boots seemed to make an awful lot of noise on the stairs, and the whole building groaned and creaked as we passed through. As we headed for the front door, I couldn't believe it wouldn't be locked, or an alarm wouldn't go off. To be honest, I half hoped it would. But I'd forgotten, the place was locked to the outside, to stop dangerous people getting in, not from the inside, to stop people getting out. This was a shelter, not a prison.

We sneaked out into a strange world. The pavements were dark, but lit in patches and pools by the streetlights. Few people seemed to

71

be about, but those who were hurried about their business with their heads down in their turned-up collars, some with umbrellas. High above us, the tall buildings pulsed out their lights—pink, gold, blue—but now the glow did not seem to get far from the windows and advertising signs before it was halted by the swirling, greenish-black storm clouds.

A moon, not quite full, flashed into view if you looked for it, just for a few seconds at a time, before another great sea of cloud swept across it again.

The wind lashed around us and snatched the breath from your mouth if you opened it to speak. Honey had pulled a dark woolen hat low over her ears, and had on a tatty but warm-looking coat. I just had my denim jacket. I shivered, pushing my hands into the pockets, and pulled my neck in, like a tortoise in his shell, but it didn't help keep the cold out. At least it had stopped raining—for now.

I trotted to keep up with Honey, though I was taller and had longer legs.

"Where are we going?" I gasped.

"Cemetery. That's where Daniel's gone. It's not far," Honey shouted back against the wind.

Great. It was turning into one of those films, all right. First mistake, getting out of bed to see about the scratching noise at the door. Now heading to a cemetery through a stormy, dark night.

But we never got there. And I was wrong. We *were* going to be in the sort of thing you see in scary films, but not the sort I'd imagined.

It all happened so quickly, but—weirdly—also in slow motion.

Honey caught sight of Daniel ahead of us and on the other side of the road.

Just for a moment he was caught in a silent flash of lightning, and I could see his trademark flop of fringe swinging wetly from beneath his hood.

He was walking with his head down, hugging the shadow of the buildings. Honey pointed silently to him and I nodded, to show I'd seen him.

The odd car passed by but there were few people about now. We were about to cross the road, when suddenly, out of nowhere, there was an insistent roar as a car engine gunned, and a loud crack of thunder. But as the thunder grumbled away, we heard the cracking sound continue—it sounded a bit like party balloons popping right by your ear.

I stopped dead, puzzled, and so did Honey. She grabbed my arm and held on so tight I felt her fingers bruising my skin through my jacket sleeve. I caught sight of Daniel sprinting to the next building, one of the big Insurance Towers he'd talked about, I now realized, with blue neon glowing from its windows and signs high up. Then he was hidden by a dark car screeching along the road which divided us. Then—more of the popping sounds, a tremendous crash of glass, and the car had gone. All that was left was a dark, wet pavement, sparkling with thousands of pieces of glass like a pool in the forest, with a small dark mound in the center of it where Daniel had been. For a moment there was no one, no sound and nothing else in the world, just my heart pounding, Honey's grip on my arm and the quiet, still little mound.

Then we heard the screaming—a woman's

high-pitched voice—and running footsteps, people we had not seen, some disappearing like liquid melting away, some running toward the glass and . . . Daniel.

"She got him!" screamed Honey, waking me from where I stood frozen to the spot.

"What?" I was confused. I wasn't sure what had just happened. I had never seen Honey anything other than calm.

"They came—the cars with the blacked-out windows, remember? He got to the best building, but where were the Angels? She got him! The Crying Lady got him! Don't you see? Look at the glass!"

Honey was hysterical.

I was still too horrified to know what to say or do.

Suddenly there was a deep voice above us.

"No, she didn't."

Honey wouldn't listen at first, and tried to run across the road to Daniel. But I looked up at the tall figure we somehow hadn't noticed, who'd left the crowd and headed to us, and saw—Joe's face.

He grabbed Honey firmly by both arms and crouched down in front of her so she wasn't going anywhere.

"Listen to me. She didn't get him," he said again, fixing her wild, sea eyes with his steady brown ones. "He caught a bullet, not a spell. From the gangsters in the car. Ambulance is on its way. He'll maybe make it yet. Just calm down. And you!" He switched his gaze to me, and his eyebrows went up nearly as high as Sarah drew hers. "What are you doing out here?"

"I—er—we were trying to bring Daniel back . . . ," I stammered.

"We didn't want him to get in trouble," explained Honey, in a brilliant return to her matter-of-fact self.

"Naturally," sighed Joe, straightening up.

A siren shrieked its opening-and-closing-mouth sound, and more people melted away as an ambulance and police cars arrived.

Joe looked over at them, then back to us.

"I'd better see you two safely back then," he said.

"What about . . . ?" I began.

"He's in good hands," said Joe. "I left him with an off-duty nurse who was passing, lucky for him, and now he'll get patched up at hospital. They are experts there," he said, and added under his breath, "Need to be, around here."

"But the . . . ," began Honey, then clammed up.

"What, this, you mean?" asked Joe, and held his big fist out to her, then slowly uncurled the gnarled fingers. In the middle of his palm lay a small, wilted leaf.

EIGHT
Joe's Secret Idea

Honey stared at the leaf, then back at Joe, but didn't say anything. I remembered what she'd said about grown-ups not understanding.

"I'm going straight to the cemetery after I've seen you back. I know which grave. The boy told me. I promised," said Joe solemnly.

Honey gazed at him, amazed.

"Come on," he said, taking each of us by a shoulder and turning us firmly back to face the way we'd come. "Let's get going. I've had a very long day, and it looks like it's going to be even longer."

We were quiet on the walk back. I think we were both silenced by Joe's kindness and common sense. He hadn't shouted and told us off *and* he was going to carry out Daniel's task, which wasn't at all what we'd expected from a grown-up. He hadn't asked who the Crying Lady was when he'd heard Honey screaming, but had just said calmly that she hadn't got Daniel after all. It was as if he knew everything already.

Feeling guilty also has a way of swallowing up any idea of words. We were thinking about Beatrice and Sarah, and I suppose Honey was thinking about her mum, and how they'd all react, and about Joe's long, hard day, which had just got longer and harder. We'd put ourselves in danger as well as not protecting Daniel, so achieved nothing by our little adventure.

A funny thing happened on the way back—I didn't think about it much at the time, but we certainly thought more about it later. As we were rounding a corner, a small, squarish figure sidestepped to avoid us. Joe muttered, "'Scuse me," and was about to pass by, when the figure peered out and up at him from under her squashy hat and said: "Ah! It's you! The gentleman who saved the little girl from the car!"

I recognized her then as the lady who had checked I was OK and then had to get back to feed Vernon, whoever he was.

Honey looked on quizzically as we all said hello,

that we were fine, and so forth; then it was my turn to wait, puzzled, as the adults suddenly went all private in their chitchat, Joe leaning down low over the lady as she muttered something to him. "Don't worry," Joe said to her, straightening up. "I'll find out."

"I expect you will," said Mrs. Vernon, as I had named her privately. "I thought it best you knew. I was hoping I'd run into you again." Joe patted her on the shoulder and we walked on.

"What was all that about?" I asked.

"Someone's been asking about you," said Joe. He kept looking ahead so I couldn't judge his expression.

"Who?" asked Honey. "Is it Lexi's family?"

"She doesn't know, exactly. Not likely to be family, as they didn't seem to have a name, just a description. Her son told her. He remembered she'd mentioned something to him about that incident with the car and me and so on the other day. He heard people in clubs and bars were asking about a stray child, fitting your description, wandered here from Sweetside. A man was offering money for information." Joe looked troubled.

"I wonder what man it is. Maybe the police?" I said.

"Police know where you are already," Joe reminded me, striding on a little faster. Rain was starting to spit lightly on our faces again.

Me and Honey panted to keep up.

"Did her son tell the people—about his mum seeing me?" I asked.

"Don't know. She said he was a bit vague about that. I think she's worried about who wants to find you and thinks her son may have talked. But don't worry. The Shelter is safe enough—so long as you are in it, of course. Save your breath and let's get a move on."

So me and Honey put our heads down and trotted every few steps to keep up with him.

I tried to make sense of Joe's mood. Why wasn't he too happy about someone trying to find me? Why was Mrs. Vernon feeling the same way? Who—or what—was I safe from, inside the Shelter?

I had to put all of this out of my head once we arrived there again. We thought there would be quite a wait after Joe rang the bell, at that time of night, but the door flew open to reveal Sarah, eyebrows practically in her hair, and Honey's mum behind her making so much noise that there wasn't really any airspace left for anyone else to shout and scream.

Beatrice luckily appeared just behind them, and in the end Honey's mum—who oddly seemed to cry and shout more, not less loudly as she realized Honey was safe and sound—had to be led away by the other women to calm down, so we were saved from a huge amount of attention for the moment.

Joe, for the first time, looked a bit rattled by this carry-on—it seemed screaming and shouting women bothered him more than gunfire—and he waited with us in the beige TV room until Sarah reappeared, as if he didn't trust us not to make a run for it if he left us alone for a moment.

He reminded me that I shouldn't be running about after a concussion and asked, Did I know what that was? I said I thought so, but except for the memory thing—which was coming back slowly—I did feel all right. Except a bit tired now.

He made a "Hrumph" sound, and looked at his watch, which I took to mean he wasn't surprised I was tired, at this time of night.

Joe knew all about concussions, it turned out, because he'd been a boxer. Me and Honey were quite interested then. We'd never met a boxer before. In fact, it isn't something you expect—it's not usually mentioned in a list of careers or jobs, it isn't what someone's dad does for a living, and you don't seem to bump into them often. We asked why he wasn't a boxer now, and he laughed and pointed out he was a little old for it, plus there was only so much a body could take.

"Anyway"—he smiled—"I am a boxer, in a way." And then added, as if it was the punch line to a joke he'd told a hundred times, "I work loading and unloading boxes."

"Oh," we both said a bit awkwardly, because his smile was sad underneath, and like all grown-ups, he didn't hide it as well as he thought he did.

"Is that what you do in both jobs?" I asked politely, because I remembered I'd been told he worked shifts at two places.

"Pretty much." He nodded. "Except sometimes I get to crush and fold empty ones, just by way of a change."

There was a bit of a silence then. Joe seemed far too clever, sensible, brave and—though strong—too *old* to be doing that sort of work, I thought. I don't know what Honey was thinking, but she seemed to think the silence needed filling, so she said brightly, "Lexi remembers Ferdy Majik, you know, Joe. We had the TV on today and you should have seen her dance!"

"Oh! Lexi, is it? You remembered your name at last? Isn't that something? I thought I couldn't go on calling you Little Miss No-Name— I'd just about decided on Nuisance." Joe smiled, and added helpfully, "After a dog I once had, you know."

Honey giggled. I shot them both an irritated but, I hope, dignified glare.

"Well, I didn't remember it on my own.

Beatrice helped—she thought she recognized me—and then I saw Ferdy—" I broke off. Joe's smile had disappeared and he was staring at me with the oddest expression. It was as if he'd just realized something, or had a fantastic idea, but on top of that—surely not—was there a hint of *fear* in his eyes?

"What?" I asked, worried. "What is it, Joe?"

He seemed to make an effort and pulled himself together.

"Nothing! Nothing . . . just . . ." He turned his gaze away from me, at the floor, at the wall. I could see he was thinking furiously, trying to make sense of something.

Then he looked back at me.

"Lexi—you said Beatrice remembered you— she reminded you of your name, right?"

"Yes. Well, she said Lexina. That didn't quite feel right to me. Then I remembered. Lexi. For short, I guess."

"Yes," said Joe impatiently. "She'd met you before then? Here?"

"She said so—or it might have been at one

of the other shelters, I don't remember. She said just once, with my gran, Myrtle." I stared at him, puzzled.

"Oh!" Joe looked surprised. "Oh, well then, that's good, that's all right. She on her way, this gran?"

"I don't know if Beatrice has actually spoken to her yet. She said she knew where she worked and was phoning . . ." I trailed off. Joe stood up, looked around as if he wanted to go, then remembered he was waiting for Sarah or Beatrice to return and paced over to the window instead. Me and Honey exchanged glances.

Just at that moment, Beatrice appeared. She had on a stern expression, but once again we were saved by an interruption from an adult.

"Ah, Beatrice," said Joe eagerly, and crossed the room to the door in two of his big strides. "Could I just have a word?" And he pointed to mean *outside the room*, so we knew he didn't want us to hear.

Beatrice had to replace the stern expression

with a nice one, as Joe had once more been a hero, but she looked across at us and faltered.

"Umm, all right, of course," she said to Joe, then to us: "Go on, you two. Honey, your mum is in the kitchen with Sarah; run along there, would you? And Lexi, straight up to bed. I'll come and check on you both in a minute. We'll have a talk about all this in the morning."

You could tell she was disappointed not to be able to give us a thorough grilling right then, but we were relieved. By the morning she wouldn't be so cross and it would be a lot easier.

We went out of the room past her without a word of complaint, with our heads down a bit, and saying "Thank you" to Joe, and "Sorry" to Beatrice, which is what you do when you realize you've got off lightly. But of course we wanted to stay and hear what they were going to talk about.

Because we'd left the room, it meant they didn't have to go somewhere else to talk now and, sure enough, we heard Beatrice say to Joe: "We can talk in here . . ." and she closed the door behind us as we walked away.

I looked at Honey and Honey looked at me.

We stopped for a moment. We looked ahead toward where the kitchen area lay, then behind us to the closed door. Without saying a word we turned and tiptoed back.

I cupped my ear and pressed close to the door. A pleasant plasticky smell floated up from the new paint. I could hear the deep rumble of Joe's voice but not what he was saying. Honey darted off and reappeared swiftly. She'd pinched a plastic cup from somewhere, and she shook out some drops of leftover drink and passed it to me.

I placed this against the door and listened again. Ah! That was better. Now I could hear words. I gave Honey the thumbs-up sign.

"I was just checking what she said was right," Joe was saying, "and I'm glad you've got it all sorted out. Silly of me—I heard the news today, like you probably did, and I got to thinking, and before you know it, you've made two and two equal five." And he chuckled.

Then came Beatrice's voice. She wasn't chuckling.

"What was on the news today? No, I didn't see it—didn't have time. Tell me."

"Well, it was nothing. Turns out you've found the girl's grandmother, is that right?" asked Joe.

"Took a bit of tracking down," said Beatrice. "But I got her at last. She's coming over tomorrow. I only just finish talking to her and lo and behold I find Lexi's gone! I was worried to death. I would have been in any case, but to think what her grandmother would have said if we'd lost her before she'd got here!" Beatrice's laugh sounded uneasy, and Joe, like me, seemed to have noticed. Honey made a face at me. She was listening too, but didn't have a cup. I gestured at her to wait.

"So, she's coming tomorrow?" he asked. "I'm surprised she ain't over here as fast as she can get here. Worried to death, she must have been." And he paused, as if waiting for something from Beatrice.

"You—you'd think so, wouldn't you?" said

Beatrice, the unease now clear in her voice. "Certainly, she sounded completely shocked. When I first told her, she started to deny it could be Lexi. Then she suddenly stopped and checked lots of details with me—Lexi's name, appearance, everything. As if she couldn't believe it."

"Oh!" came Joe's voice. "Just grateful, I suppose. Never dreamt someone would find her this quick. She's the child's only relative?"

Honey looked up and down the hall to check if anyone was coming. She was almost hopping with exasperation, because she couldn't hear what was being said. I waved at her to go on, I'd tell her all later; I was worried that if she hung around, Sarah and her mother would come looking. She sidled off reluctantly toward the kitchen, throwing wistful looks over her shoulder as she went.

"Yes, so far as I know," Beatrice was saying. "Mother died when Lexi was just a baby—she was single—so the grandmother was left to bring her up alone. It's been hard on her. I know she's worked two jobs for years to keep the two of them.

But when I met her, she seemed very fond of the child, and wasn't complaining. I just wonder . . ."

"What?" asked Joe.

"Oh, I don't know. Whether it's all been a bit too much for her," said Beatrice awkwardly. "You see, she said some odd things."

"How do you mean, odd things?" prompted Joe.

"Obviously I asked when and how she'd lost Lexi, and she first denied she had—until I made it clear we'd found her—then she never did explain. It was as if she wasn't sure how it had happened. Then, of course, like you said, you'd think she'd race straight over here. Even if she was working, surely her boss would let her come for something so important."

"Well, what did she say about coming?"

"She started to say she'd be straight over, then said, Oh of course, she'd have to find someone to mind Lexina while she came. I had to remind her *we* were minding the child!"

"It does sound like maybe she's getting a bit tired," agreed Joe. "Age catches up with all of us. Perhaps she could just do with a little help in the future."

"Mm," said Beatrice. "She's entitled, at her age. Anyway, what was this story on the news I missed? And what does it have to do with Lexi?"

"Nothing, nothing. Like I said, two and two making five. Never was that good at school," said Joe, and I could hear him smiling through the words.

"Mind if I come around when Myrtle shows up?" he added casually. "I love a happy reunion."

"I should hope you *will* be there!" answered Beatrice. "Myrtle will want to thank you— twice over!"

Joe started making embarrassed sounds, and I suddenly realized the voices were growing louder. They must be moving toward the door.

I snatched the cup away and hurtled up the corridor and the stairs before they could see me.

I got into bed as fast as I could, and practically suffocated myself trying to quiet my breathing—my heart was racing in my chest—as I heard Beatrice downstairs showing Joe out, little knowing he was on his way to do his duty at the cemetery for Daniel. I looked at my watch. Nearly two in the morning. Poor Joe, I thought. At least the storm seemed to have passed.

And I lay there fretting, knowing Beatrice was coming to check on me, Honey would be itching to know what I'd overheard, Daniel was possibly dying in hospital and, once again, I fell asleep worrying about a grandmother I still didn't remember, who sounded like she had her own memory problems.

That night I dreamt restlessly, seeing Daniel's huddled figure, but now he was somehow lying on the surface of a pool, in the middle of the forest, and the water was deep and dark, so I didn't know how to reach him. I was scared he would drown, as I couldn't see how he was staying up on the surface of the water, not exactly floating in it, lying just as solidly as he had on the glittering pavement in the dark night. And then I saw the bird, the one I'd seen in the forest, glittering amethyst and emerald, its beak flashing red, tipped yellow, and it picked its way across the surface to Daniel on its long yellow legs, as if to say: *Look, it's all right, I can do it, Daniel is safe.*

It didn't make any sense at all but, for some reason, I was calmed completely, and felt sure Daniel would be all right.

NINE
Myrtle's Secret

In the morning, when I woke up, there was good news and bad news.

The good news was that Beatrice had phoned the hospital in the night and found out Daniel was going to make it. He'd been lucky, she said. A bullet had passed right through the side of him, and although he was a skinny kid it seemed to have missed everything important. I asked, Who would shoot at a nine-year-old boy? Beatrice said they weren't trying to shoot him, they were people fighting with other people, and just weren't particularly careful about anyone who happened to be in the way.

I mulled this over, and thought it was odd that a grown-up would call Daniel "lucky," considering. People shooting at other people and accidentally getting someone else—even a little kid? You could understand how Honey and Daniel's story—the Crying Lady, or the Scarlet Prince's bad angels or whatever they were, trying to get children and ordinary people, *on purpose,* in their battle for control—almost seemed to make more sense.

The bad news was, Honey had gone. It didn't take much, apparently, to spook her mum, and last night's events had been enough to make her bolt early in the morning, back out to the streets, perhaps on to another shelter.

The other thing which struck me, as soon as I was out of bed and down the stairs, was that there seemed to be more people about—and more arriving all the time. They were all different ages and types, but they shared a similar look. Bulky clothes in layers, to keep out the cold. Everything shabby except for a brand-new coat, or trainers, or shoes, which looked a bit strange with the rest of their clothes. Over breakfast, I asked Beatrice why they'd all suddenly appeared.

"Usually, we are always busy. You turned up when we'd just reopened after decorating the place. We were given some paint and chairs and so on—people get leftover stuff and give it to us—so we thought we'd do it properly for once. I think people didn't realize we'd opened again for a day or two."

"Oh," I said, and added politely, "It looks very nice." Though actually I thought some of the colors were a bit strange, and the chairs, as I've told you, were pretty awful to use. I munched a bit of toast.

"Yes," said Beatrice in a tired way. "Always too many. Just want somewhere for a day or two, most of them, and something hot to eat, plus we give out warm clothes and shoes which are donated. We usually have to turn people away. Not enough room."

"But it's a huge building!" I said, then had to say sorry for spraying toast crumbs everywhere.

Beatrice laughed.

"It is, you're right. But we only have the ground and first floor, haven't you noticed? The rest is a wreck. We don't have the money to turn that into anything we can use. Everything you see here—and don't forget the beds, and the laundry bills, and the food—kind people give us. Charity only goes so far."

"That's a shame," I said. "All this big building empty, and people sleeping out on the streets. It doesn't make sense."

"Lots of things are like that," sighed Beatrice, rubbing her cropped head, "but at least the folks who give us money and things are trying." It didn't suit her face to look sad, and it didn't stay that way long. She smiled at me. "Anyway, look sharp and tidy yourself up today. Myrtle is coming at eleven o'clock!"

Maybe something showed in my face, because she leant in close to me—there were quite a few people around at the tables today—and said, "Are you worried—about meeting her?"

I nodded.

"Why?" she asked simply.

"I don't remember her. She might be a bit upset. Also, I don't know what she's like. I mean, will I just have to go with her—straightaway?" I mumbled somewhere in the direction of my plate.

I felt the palm of Beatrice's hand, leathery but

warm and gentle, beneath my chin, as she tilted my face up so that I had to look at her.

"Don't you worry about that. First of all, I bet if you know her, you'll recognize her straightaway—just like Ferdy Majik on the TV. Second, we are going to make sure that wherever you go, you are going to be safe and happy. All right?" Her cloudy brown eyes held mine.

"All right," I said. "Thanks, Beatrice."

But I couldn't help thinking of Honey. Was she safe and happy? No one here seemed to have had any say when her mother took her away.

It was an age till eleven o'clock.

I scrubbed at my boots with an old nail brush I found by the sink in one of the toilets, and made them look a bit better and the nail brush a whole lot worse. I rinsed it as best I could and put the sink plug on top of it to hide it a bit. I asked Sarah for a comb, which was a big mistake, as she then set about my hair with one which felt as if it had been sharpened, and showed no mercy, even when I shrieked. When I looked in the mirror afterward, scalp smarting and eyes watering, I saw she'd managed to make a sort of parting and put in two bunches, and although the bands were too tight it did look quite good.

Then I put on my denim jacket, which Beatrice had thoughtfully dried from its soaking in the storm, and went to wait in the TV room, but there were two old men watching the racing and a younger man who was muttering to himself, so I skulked up the stairs to my bedroom to wait and hoped Joe would turn up.

I sat on my bed and wished I had a book to read. I thought about Daniel, and hoped maybe I'd be allowed to visit him soon. But I wouldn't be able to visit Honey so easily. I was just feeling a bit sorry for myself when, at five to eleven, Sarah tapped at the door and told me Joe was downstairs in the TV room, and Myrtle would be arriving any minute.

When I got down there, the other people had gone and Joe was sitting in an armchair. He looked very tired, which wasn't surprising, I suppose. A big smile crinkled his face, though, and again I thought how it could make you feel like you do when the sunshine suddenly comes out on a rotten gray day, and I just had to smile right back.

"You heard about Daniel?" I asked him.

"Yes. I'm hoping to get to see him soon, put his mind at ease," said Joe.

"You took the leaf?" I asked. "Did you really? Or will you just tell him you did?"

"I did really," sighed Joe, rubbing a great paw across his eyes. "I could have just thrown it away, of course, and told him I'd delivered it and, if he didn't know, what would be the harm? But I am someone who can rest easier at night if I do what I promise and tell the truth."

"But—do you know why he wanted you to do that?" I pressed.

"Of course. His dead brother's spirit has to get to the forest."

"Honey said—she said not to talk to grown-ups about stuff like that. And the Warrior Angels, and the Crying Lady. But do you know all about it already?"

"I know all about it," said Joe.

To my surprise, he suddenly looked very serious, sat up, leant toward me and wagged a forefinger at me as he spoke.

"And by the way, for children, there's one very important rule to stick to, and you listen well, Lexi. If anyone ever tells you not to tell grown-ups something, you can bet you probably ought to tell them. Try not to promise not to tell, but if you do, it's one of the few promises you're allowed to break. Children are one thing—if they say it, you listen up and decide yourself if you should tell a grown-up. If the kid might be unhappy or in danger, you have to tell. But a grown-up—you ever have one of those telling you not to tell other grown-ups something—that's when you really want to watch out. You ask yourself, Why would they want to keep whatever it is secret? You tell a grown-up you trust, always. Got that?"

I stared at him, amazed. I saw he was waiting, with his kind eyes now fixed and keen as a dog on a scent.

I nodded.

Joe relaxed again and sat back in his chair.

"Secrets," he said, "can be dangerous. Usually better out than in, I find."

I nodded again. My throat had gone a bit dry. I cleared it before managing to say what I'd wanted to ask.

"And—and what do you think? About the stories?"

"What do I *think*? What do you mean?"

"Well, I mean, do you think they're true? Or just silly?" I felt silly now, asking.

Joe looked at the ceiling for a moment, with his forefingers touched together like a steeple, considering.

"I don't think they're silly, no. True? Well, that all depends where you're looking from, doesn't it?"

And then there was the sound of the front door buzzer, out in the hall—then the clunks of the locks and door handle; Beatrice's voice, a sudden silence, then someone else's, quieter, old; finally, a bustling of coats and a shuffle of shoes.

I stiffened and waited, looking toward the door. It opened slightly but no one came in.

"Perhaps I should—" we heard Beatrice saying,

her voice sounding worried, then another muttered exchange with the quiet voice just beyond the door. I shot a glance at Joe, but didn't want to miss anything. He, too, was staring fixedly at the half-open door.

At last, Beatrice appeared, with the strangest expression on her face, and looked at me.

"Lexi—this is Myrtle."

She stood aside, and an old lady, leaning on a cane, stepped into the room almost shyly. She was shorter than Beatrice, thin as a rail, in a patterned blue dress and flat shoes, with short, curly gray hair which was almost white in places, and her eyes sought mine, desperate, eager, but worried. My first feeling was relief, because I instantly liked her, in that strange way you can't control. A second feeling of awkwardness—because I honestly didn't recognize her—was only just starting to well up, when it was well and truly whacked out of the way by a third feeling of complete shock at what came next.

Beatrice, looking helpless, added from behind her, "And this is—er, this is—"

"Lexina," said the old lady in her careful, small voice. She stepped aside, and there in the doorway was a girl.

I recognized her, of course. She'd been in every mirror I had ever looked into.

TEN
Myrtle Explains

We stood there, staring at each other, for about ten seconds. The weird thing was, would you believe it, she even had her hair done just like Sarah had done mine.

Joe was the first to break the silence.

"Wow," he said from behind me.

Then he was at my side. I wasn't looking at him, or anyone else, because my eyes were glued to the image of myself standing uncertainly in the doorway, but I felt him there.

"Lexina," he said, and held out his hand toward her. "How lovely to meet you. I am Joe, and this here is Lexi."

Lexina dragged her eyes from mine, managed a smile and timidly shook Joe's bear paw.

Trust Joe to do the right thing. Suddenly I realized I had been staring rudely at this girl without saying a word—though of course, she'd been staring back at me, just as shocked as I was by the look

of things. How must *she* feel? Same as me, I supposed. Like someone had stolen your identity—
how dare someone else look just like you?—mixed
with a strange feeling of having known each other
for years. I had needed so badly to recognize
someone—and here it was, handed to me on a
plate. My own self.

I smiled as best I could and held out my
hand like Joe, but more scared, I bet, than he felt.
Would she hate me and refuse to shake? Would it
feel like touching a mirror if she did? Perhaps she
wasn't real. . . .

"Hi, Lexina," I squeaked. I didn't know what
had happened to my real voice.

I think I was a bit slower on the uptake than
everyone else.

Lexina smiled back at me, grabbed my hand and
squeezed it—and her hand felt real and warm. The
startled expression left her eyes and a special look
came into them—friendship, hope, love—and
the strangest thing was, I could feel it happening
to me at the same time, these feelings rushing all
over me and showing back at her in my eyes.

She suddenly dragged me by my hand toward her and threw her arms around me, and I did the same, though I didn't understand anything, and we hugged, and started to sniff with tears, then pulled our heads away a little to look at each other again close up, and Lexina laughed, and I laughed too, and we hugged again.

"Two peas in a pod," said Beatrice, and I could hear tears in her voice, although she was laughing, and Joe just kept saying:

"Will you look at that. Will you look at that!"

Well, the moment came when we stepped apart, but still holding hands, and then I realized everyone else was looking at Myrtle in a waiting sort of way.

She stood looking very small, older and more fragile than before, and she was sniffing and dabbing tears with a tissue, but she wasn't smiling or laughing. She looked very unhappy. Lexina put a hand out to her and grabbed her arm.

"Gran! Don't cry!"

She even sounded just like me. Well, what did I expect?

Beatrice was at the old lady's side in a second, with an arm around her shoulders, and lots of kind noises, and we all followed to gather around as Beatrice helped her to an armchair. At that moment, Sarah peered in.

Joe glanced over at her.

"Some tea might be an idea, Sarah, if you have time," he said gently. Sarah took in the scene for a moment and, looking more surprised than ever, did a double take, then shot swiftly away toward the kitchen without a word.

While we were waiting for Myrtle to gather herself together, me and Lexina couldn't keep our eyes off each other.

"How . . . ?" I said weakly. "Why . . . ?"

Lexina whispered, "You're my twin. I mean, I'm your twin. I mean, we're twins!" And she grinned and hopped up and down on the spot.

"Did you two know each other *before?*" asked Joe, hitting the nail on the head as usual.

"No," said Lexina.

"Even Lexina didn't know she had a sister. Let alone a twin. Till this morning," came Myrtle's quavering voice suddenly. We looked at her. She blew her nose.

"It's true," said Lexina, looking at Joe, then back at me. "Gran was acting all strange yesterday evening, and she wouldn't tell me what was wrong. Then this morning she said it was no good, she'd got something to tell me. And this was it. I mean, that I had a twin sister I'd never known about, and we were going to meet her."

She stopped suddenly and looked at me.

"Did *you* know?"

"I had no idea," I said. "No one told me. I'm fairly sure it wasn't something I knew before I hit my head."

"But you knew before I came?"

"No. I was just waiting to see my gran. Myrtle. Beatrice thought she remembered me with her. But . . ."

Beatrice groaned and put her hand to her forehead.

"So I was remembering *Lexina*," she said. "This explains a lot. Like Myrtle saying she had to find someone to mind Lexina if she came over here.

Lexi, Lexina—I thought they were one and the same person. I didn't understand what she was talking about."

Lexina gasped, and turned to me.

"You mean the first you knew of it was when you *saw* me? What a shock! I mean, it was a shock for me in any case!" She turned and looked at Myrtle. "Gran! Why didn't you *warn* her? Them?" she added, waving around to include Beatrice and Joe.

This was the first glimpse I had of how caring and thoughtful my twin was—much more so than me.

Myrtle was cowering slightly in her chair. I could feel Beatrice and Joe were thinking the same thing as Lexina.

"I—I couldn't be sure. I just didn't believe it. Then I heard the news story and it all started to make sense," she quavered.

That news story again! I shot Joe a look, but he showed no expression.

Sarah appeared with a tray full of cups of strong tea.

111

"I took one look at all of you and thought everyone could do with one," she explained, and plonked the tray down on the table, adding, "and one for me while I get over the shock. Let me look at you two a moment." And she stood there, shaking her head, comparing, her eyes flitting back and forth.

"Doesn't seem right," she announced finally, to no one in particular, "that so few of us are blessed with good looks, and then whoever's in charge of such things goes and doles it out to two of them at the same time."

Me and Lexina shuffled our feet a bit and grinned at each other, and the grown-ups chuckled—even Myrtle—and Sarah handed round the cups of tea, and we all pulled armchairs up close to Myrtle's and sat down.

After a few quiet sips, Myrtle spoke up.

"I've been a very foolish old woman, as you can all tell."

Beatrice and Joe made "No, no" noises. Sarah didn't know what was going on, so said nothing.

"I had better explain—to all of you, but especially to the girls."

"Can I ask something?" I put in. I had just thought of something worrying.

"Of course," said Myrtle.

"If Lexina is Lexina, then—*who am I*? I mean, what is my name? I thought I was Lexi, short for Lexina. But if she's . . ."

Myrtle waved at me to stop and I trailed off.

"It's all right, Lexi. You *are* Lexi. You *did* remember right. Lexi and Lexina. That's what your mother named you both. A pair"—and now she sniffed again and had to put down her cup of tea and take a tissue from Beatrice—"and I should never have let you be parted."

Lexina threw me a look. It said, *Please forgive her.* I gave her a tiny nod to show I understood.

Myrtle went on:

"Your mother, my daughter Maria, she left you both in my care when she died. Now, she had been going out with your father for quite some time before she came to be expecting you. He was just a poor boy from around here, as we are, but he was honest and smart and he worked hard. But then he started to do well and became more successful. His work took him away more and more. Maria—rightly or wrongly—felt that she didn't know him anymore, that maybe he felt she wasn't good enough for him now. He saw less of her because he wasn't around so much, but she thought maybe it was because he didn't *want* to see her. Why didn't he take her with him, to these important business meetings?

"Well, who knows now what he felt, or who was right; it's none of our business. The truth is, the two of them rowed and that was it, all over. Maria said she'd have the baby—as she thought it was then, she had no idea it was twins—and manage on her own and he wasn't to come back, she wanted nothing more to do with him. I tried to reason with her, but . . ." Myrtle trailed off and looked sadly into her tea, as if she were watching all the events there.

"So Maria's baby turns out to be *babies*! Twins, especially for a first-time mother—well, that's quite a handful. She moved in with me and we did our best to manage on just my wages when Maria couldn't work anymore. She worked right up till the last moment, though. I said to her, 'But their father is doing well now. He can provide!' But she was very proud." She sighed and shook her head.

"How . . . how did Maria—my mother, I mean our mother—die?" I asked. I felt it was something I needed to know, however painful it might be.

Myrtle looked at me and spoke gently.

"She died when you were both only a few months old. She was on her way back from a shift at the factory while I minded you. She was crossing the road—a car hit her and didn't stop. It was a getaway car, from a robbery, they think. They didn't ever catch them."

Myrtle's blue patterned dress rustled in the silence; someone patted my arm; Joe sighed.

"But how did we come to be split up? Couldn't you afford to keep us both?" asked Lexina.

"No, no," said Myrtle. "It wasn't that. It was hard, I admit, but I'd have done anything to keep you both. It was your father."

"My—our—father?" I asked.

Myrtle nodded so that her frosty curls bobbed.

"He heard—I don't know how, maybe saw a newspaper report—about Maria's death and somehow he tracked me down. I came to the door—I remember it to this day—with you in my arms, Lexi. You'd just woken up, and I didn't want you to wake Lexina as well; she was still asleep in the bed.

"He said he'd heard about Maria and he was sorry. He was upset. He said he'd come for the baby."

"The *baby?*" put in Lexina. Myrtle shook her head and sobbed.

"He didn't know, of course. He didn't know there were two. How could he? He'd left before Maria herself knew. I didn't know what to do. He was the father. He did have the right. He did have all a child could want or need—and what was I? A very poor old lady, who could hardly keep herself, let alone a child, and might drop down dead at any moment! No security, no future for a child. That's what it would have looked like to a court, if it had come to that.

"But still, I had promised Maria as she lay dying"—and here her voice broke and she struggled before going on—"to look after the babies. So . . . so I handed the baby—you, Lexi—over. And I said nothing about Lexina. I thought, maybe this way I'm still keeping my promise—to look after the babies—and doing right by their father. I didn't lie to him. I thought, if Lexina wakes, and cries, then it's a sign. He will hear it and the truth will be out, and both will go to their father, and what will be, will be."

Now Myrtle looked to Lexina. "But I prayed you wouldn't wake, Lexina, I admit it. I loved you both the same"—she looked to me and grabbed my hand and held it tight—"and as much as I had loved my own daughter. I could hardly stand to let *one* of you go. Already, as you left my arms, Lexi, it felt like one half of my heart was being torn away. If I'd lost you both, I don't think I could have lived. With Maria gone, what else was there to live for? What use is an old woman, with no one left who loves her, and with no one left to love?"

And with that, she gave in to tears completely, and so did pretty well all the rest of us, I think.

What with all the sniffing, and comforting, and arms around each other, we never had time to get to another important bit in Myrtle's tale—which would have saved a terrible lot of bother—because Sarah heard the front-door buzzer and trotted off to see who it was.

We heard her ask someone to wait; then she appeared all jittery in the doorway and looked distractedly from Myrtle to Beatrice.

"What is it?" asked Beatrice.

"Well, I hardly know—it's not what, it's who," said Sarah.

"What on earth's the matter with you, Sarah?" said Beatrice, exasperated, rising to her feet. "Who, then?"

"It's a gentleman. He—he says he's Lexi's father."

ELEVEN
The Blue Lady

"It *can't* be," said Myrtle.

"It *can't* be," said Joe, just a fraction of a second behind her.

All of us looked at them, Myrtle looked at Joe in surprise, and Joe looked solidly back at Myrtle. Sarah looked from one to the other of them for explanation, then to Beatrice, for instruction.

This second delay was to prove disastrous.

The next moment, there was a slight tap at the half-open door behind her, and a tall man in a dark suit shouldered his way into the room. Sarah had to come further in to get out of his way.

Everyone had risen half out of their chairs and we all froze like that. He was a middle-aged man, with neat, short-cropped hair, and he was smiling in a hopeful sort of way. His eyes scanned around us, and came to rest on me and Lexina. Then his eyebrows went up and he took another look. The eyebrows lowered to a frown.

Myrtle, gripping her stick tightly, began, "Excuse me, young man, you must be mistaken—" but Joe suddenly talked over her.

"I'm sure we can sort this all out." And he stood aside from his armchair, smiling and gesturing rather grandly, like a waiter, for the man to sit there. "If Mr.—uh, I don't think we had your name, sir?"

Joe's charm worked. The man, almost scowling, seemed to remember his manners, and smiled again easily.

"Jones," he said rapidly. "Mr. Jones." He made as if to hold out his hand to Joe, but Joe seemed not to see it, as he was turning away to pull up another chair.

Mr. Jones put his hand back in his pocket awkwardly and picked through our seats to take the one Joe had offered him. Somehow Joe got in the way of me and Lexina as we were going to retake our seats, and Sarah and he took those, so we ended up in the chairs closer to the open door.

Beatrice didn't say a word, but stared coolly at the newcomer. Myrtle shrank slightly in her chair, looking smaller than ever. Sarah sat clasping her hands anxiously. Between us all, there seemed to be a silent agreement to let Joe take charge.

"Now, Mr. Jones," he said calmly. "It's quite a gathering here today. You've surprised us. Sarah said you claim to be Lexi's father—is that so?"

"There's no 'claim' about it," said Mr. Jones, a touch of irritation creeping into his smooth voice. A muscle in his jaw twitched. I stared. There was something familiar about that twitch. If I could just remember . . .

"We live at Sweetside. I said Lexi could just ride her bike for five minutes. The next thing I know, she's not back, and I'm worried sick." He looked across at me—then his eyes flickered uncertainly to Lexina.

"She was always trying to sneak off to the forest—it's not far—and I think she must have taken the bike in there and had an accident."

In the pause which followed, I think we all started to realize a few things. One—he wasn't asking how come his daughter appeared to have a double and Two—he didn't seem to be sure which

121

one of us was his darling daughter Lexi, despite the fact I was wearing the clothes I'd turned up at the Shelter in and Three—he hardly seemed to be overcome with emotion at finding said daughter, throwing his arms around her neck etc.

Thing number Four might not have seemed important to anyone else, even if they'd noticed. Joe stared at me, then looked at the man's boots. I followed his glance.

The boots were of snakeskin: deep, dull red.

My heart went *thunk* in my chest.

As naturally as I could, I took Lexina's hand and said, "Come on, let's go and get a drink while everyone talks," and she looked a bit surprised but stood up with me, and we turned to the open door.

Then all hell let loose.

We heard Myrtle give a little shriek, a chair scraped back, and a voice said menacingly, "Stop right there. No one's going anywhere. Which one of you is Lexi?"

I half turned and caught a glimpse of the man on his feet, but what was in sharp focus was the ugly, dark barrel of a gun. Then I heard Joe shout,

"GO!" and it was like an electric shock. I sprinted for the door, dragging Lexina by the hand, all the time listening for the terrible sharp cracking sound, the whistle of the bullet.

But then we were through the door and then— where to go? Front door would take too long to open—so, up the stairs, as fast as our feet could go, hearing a commotion behind us, and not sure what was happening, just knowing we had to get away, get to somewhere safe.

And where do you go, when you are scared? I didn't know anywhere else. I grabbed the door of my tiny yellow bedroom, the only place I'd felt safe, and shoved Lexina ahead of me and through it.

Lexina practically crashed onto the bed as I slammed the door and leant on it. Gasping for breath, I realized the danger we were in—we needed something more than me to hold the door shut.

"Lexina! Quick! The bed—against the door. Help me!"

Lexina jumped off and grabbed the headboard. It was very difficult, as the room was so small there wasn't really room for both of us to stand and push the bed around, but between us we managed to get the foot of the bed against the door.

The only place left to hide was crouched down between the headboard and the little window. That way we could also try our best to add our weight, leaning as hard as we could to press the bed against the door.

We cowered there, shaking in terror. We could hear footsteps running, shouting, but no gun-shots . . . yet.

I realized what a terrible situation we were now in; the defense was the best I could think of, but there was no way, if the gunman came through that door, that either of us could get past him, and the window was too small to squeeze through. We were like rats in a trap.

Lexina started to sob.

"Who is he? What does he want?" she wailed.

"Shhh," I said, and clung to her tightly. "I don't know, but he's bad news. Try and be quiet. He might not have seen where we went."

Lexina bravely swallowed her sobs and wiped her eyes.

Then she paused from her wiping and I saw she was staring at something below my chin.

"What?" I whispered.

"You—you've got a chain. Like mine." And she pulled at it.

"Yes. I've always had it. It's a—"

"Key," she breathed, laying it in her hand. "A silver key!"

"It's not that amazing, Lexina. It's only silver. Maybe now isn't the best time—get a grip on the bed in case."

"But I've got the *locket*!" she hissed excitedly. "The locket which needs the *key*! I've never been able to open it to see what's inside!"

We stared at each other.

It wasn't the time. Maybe, though, at the back of our minds, was the thought that there might never be another time, that this might be the end for both of us.

"Show me," I said.

Lexina fumbled, pulled at the chain inside her fleece top, and brought out the locket. It was small, without decoration, and the silver was blackening.

125

"There," she said, pointing to a little hole at the top of it. "That's the lock. Should I take it off?"

"Let's see, we might not need to," I said.

The chains were short but, almost nose to nose, Lexina held the locket steady and I tried to put the tiny key into the lock. It fit. A quick turn and: "That's it! I felt it! I think it will open now," said Lexina.

At that moment, the door handle rattled and we felt a thud as the door hit the other end of the bed.

I dropped the key and grabbed the wooden headboard.

"Push! Lexina, push back!"

Lexina was a smart girl. In the tiny space we had, she turned and put her back against the headboard and, with her knees bunched up under her chin, she braced her feet against the wall.

"Good idea," I said, but there didn't seem to be room for me to turn and do the same.

Thump! went the door again, and this time, the headboard jumped back violently and smacked me on the chin.

"Ouch!" I said. Angry now, as well as scared, I leant as hard as I could on the headboard. I realized Lexina was fumbling around with the locket.

"Lexina!" I said. "Not *now*! Later! Push as hard as you can!"

"Then WHEN?" shouted Lexina. "I've waited for *years* to see what's inside, and there might not *be* a later."

She was right. *Thump*—the bed crushed us further against the wall, and the door was already part open.

I heard her gasp.

"Look, Lexi! LOOK!"

I glanced over to her trembling, outstretched palm on top of her knees, now almost level with her nose.

The locket lay open. Inside was a photograph—a beautiful young woman, the kindest eyes, the proudest smile, with a tiny baby on each arm.

"It's *Mother*," I gasped. "It's Maria, our *mother*!"

"It's us," said Lexina in wonderment. "Us and our mother!"

And then the bed jolted back so hard Lexina

was almost folded into the wall, and both of us screamed. The dark-suited shoulder was through the door—now he had it completely open, and the rest of him followed swiftly. In a flash, he jumped on the bed and held the gun, quivering, toward us. The hateful red snakeskin boots were right at my eye level.

Now his face was a mask of fury.

"Which one of you is Lexi? Which *one?*" he roared.

Terror swamped us; crushed and unable to get away, we screamed. And I don't know why, maybe it was something to do with the locket, but in our moment of complete desperation, when we thought it was our last second on earth, we screamed the cry of all baby animals who need protection:

"MOTHER! MOTHER! MOTHER!"

The gun faltered, swung from me to Lexina and back again.

And then she came.

In a blur of tears, I saw her.

She appeared behind him in the doorway, a

haze of blue, floating, it seemed, with a white light around her head, and she had a magic staff in her hand, and she raised it up, and she struck, she struck him down. It was the Blue Lady. We had called her true name. And she saved us.

TWELVE
Dad

The man who called himself Mr. Jones went down with a crash.

His chin landed *smack* on the headboard, right in front of me, so that his face was up close and his eyes, open but seeing nothing, stared into mine.

Then Joe was in the doorway, filling it with his big shoulders; he grabbed the man's ankles and jerked him backward so that his head fell from the headboard onto the pillow, and in a flash, the big old boxer was on top of him, snatching the gun from his limp hand and bundling his arms behind his back.

He needn't have panicked, it turned out. The guy was out for the count and going nowhere.

Lexina managed to twist herself round and together we peered out over the headboard.

There was Joe, sitting on top of the man, and calling behind him for electrical wire or tape NOW. In the doorway, we could see Myrtle, calling for both of us, and Beatrice and Sarah trying to comfort her and push in for a view at the same time.

Behind them, it turned out, were loads of the other shelter visitors who'd heard the commotion and were all trying to find out what was happening. Someone had called the police—Beatrice, we heard later, always one to keep her head in a crisis—and they had quite a job clearing a way through the corridor and getting to the room.

By the time they did, Joe had tied the man's ankles and wrists with a great deal of washing line, which was all Sarah could find. No one could find anything to cut it with in a hurry, so there were great coils of it all round him. Joe, still sitting on him, looked over at me and grinned.

"What do you reckon, Lexi? In the river again?"

Lexina looked at me in horror, then back to Joe.

"He got out of there last time, didn't he?" I said. "I think he'd be better in jail."

Then the police were in the doorway, and as they were all pretty big it took quite a bit of shuffling and standing back to let one of them in, to drag Mr. Jones out.

Then me and Lexina realized we could get out at last, and suddenly couldn't wait, so we climbed over the bed and rushed into the corridor, and stretched and yelped and jumped about and hugged each other, and then Myrtle and Sarah and Beatrice in turn. Joe had gone with the police to explain what had happened.

Lexina hadn't been able to see, with her back to the bed, so she was trying to get me to explain how Mr. Jones had ended up knocked out cold.

"Was it Joe?" she gasped excitedly. "Did he get him?"

I wasn't sure what to say, given what I'd seen.

"It was Myrtle!" shrieked Sarah, to my amazement. "What a marvel! Some gran you've got here, you pair!" And she hugged the old lady's shoulders till she nearly took her off her feet.

"Myrtle!" I said. "I thought—I thought . . ."

"It's true!" said Beatrice. "She was up out of her chair and after him quicker than any of us! Joe reached him just at the doorway, and got him round the neck and almost had him on the floor. Joe made a grab for the gun, but the man threatened to shoot him, and whacked Joe on the side of the head with it, and left him on the floor."

"I *knew* something held him up a bit!" I said. "It gave us just enough time!"

"Then Myrtle was after him, and Sarah was trying to stop her, or get after you two, I'm not sure . . ."

"Both," put in Sarah. "Though what good I could do, I didn't know, against a gun . . ."

"And I raced to phone the police, who might be better at that," went on Beatrice, "and then dashed up in time to see Myrtle in action!"

She paused for breath.

"How—how did you . . . ?" asked Lexina, flinging her arms around Myrtle.

"She made to whack at him with her stick . . . ," began Sarah excitedly.

"But it was no good, because he was tall and up high on the bed, and I was too small; I could only hit his legs," Myrtle explained calmly, wiping tears from Lexina's cheeks, and reaching out to put her arm around me. "And I heard you both scream

133

out—for your mother, for Maria, who couldn't help you—but I thought, *I* can. I *must*. I *promised*. And it just came to me in a flash."

"So she turned the stick around," said Beatrice, taking up the story and acting it out for us, "and used the *curved* end, and hooked it round his leg and jerked *so hard*, like this"—she demonstrated with her imaginary stick—"you wouldn't believe it! And *down* he went, and *whack* went his chin . . . !"

"OH!" said me and Lexina together at the same time. So that was what had happened. Not quite what I'd thought, but still, a lady in blue had saved us, however you looked at it.

"But why did he want Lexi?" asked Lexina suddenly. "Who was he?"

"I think Joe knows," said Myrtle, giving us both a squeeze. "I certainly don't. I just know he's not your father. So I knew he was a liar before he even came in the room."

The police had cleared the corridor, but now they had gone, people were starting to gather around our little group, asking questions, trying to hug us and Myrtle, or shake her hand, even though they didn't know us.

Beatrice suddenly looked at Sarah, and they got all businesslike.

"Come on, let's get you down to the TV lounge again, and we can all have a sit-down and a cup of tea," said Beatrice, and they made a fuss of helping Myrtle, who'd just felled a large gunman, but me and Lexina knew that they were right, as shock probably isn't good for old ladies. After the excitement and terror, when we thought about what had just happened, both of us started to feel a bit wobbly too.

When we got down to the TV room—Beatrice and Sarah stopping from time to time to reassure people that the gunman was caught and everyone was safe—we found Joe and two policemen there.

The police wanted all our statements before we could get to talk to Joe, so we had to do that first, one at a time, which took ages. The policeman who took mine was very interested when, after he'd asked if I'd ever seen the man before, I told him about the man I'd met at Sweetside, who I

135

thought was the same person. He said "Aha!" and raised his eyebrows and chewed the end of his pen.

At last, they left us all to be alone together, and Joe had waited to talk to us, though he kept worrying that he might lose his job for not turning up. Sarah said, "Hrmph! We'll see about that," and went off to phone wherever it was he worked, saying, "They should be proud to have a hero working for them . . ." as she went.

Joe shook his head at us from his armchair, looking exhausted, and started to explain that Myrtle was the one who had saved the day, but we butted in with our questions.

"How did you know he couldn't be our father? Before you knew his name, or saw him?" I asked.

"Because your father is dead," said Joe heavily to me and Lexina, and added, "I'm sorry, both of you."

We turned to Myrtle.

"He's right, I'm afraid," agreed Myrtle, with a little nod of her curls. "Though how he worked it out . . . But what I want to know is what the man was thinking of, coming here after Lexi like that!"

Beatrice and Sarah now joined Myrtle, me and Lexina in staring expectantly at Joe.

"He saw the news, same as I did, and he got to thinking," said Joe. "They had a small piece on at the end, the other day, just local news, saying they were trying to track a missing child, name Lexi Jones, with a photo—old, so she was much younger, blurry, but still—I thought I recognized it."

"Jones?" I said. "Is that my name? Is that why he . . ."

"Called himself Mr. Jones, yes," answered Joe.

"Why would he pretend he was a missing child's father?" began Lexina.

"To kidnap her. Because he, like me, had put this little tucked-away story of yet another missing child together with a much bigger story from the last couple of days," said Joe, leaning forward in his chair. "Ferdy Majik dies in a car crash. Now, it's not talked about much, but every real fan knows Ferdy has a daughter. He's been determined to keep her out of the spotlight, mainly because he knows only too well the kidnappers round here target the kids of the rich and famous. So no one's allowed to photograph the kid, education takes place at home and so on, and it's worked very well. Most people have forgotten he had a daughter, if they knew in the first place.

"I noticed on the news footage of the crash scene that there were a heck of a lot of police combing through the forest from the edge of the road. As the car hit a tree right by the side of the road, it seemed a little odd to me that they were going in so deep for 'evidence.' Seemed more like they were looking for someone. Maybe someone who'd got thrown out.

"I got to thinking about it, and I started to wonder. What would they do if they thought the child was in the car, and they couldn't find the body? Looked as though the kid must have been thrown clear, was dazed, and wandered off. It would be tricky to announce it on the TV. Every kidnapper in or out of the city would turn up, hoping to grab her. Father's dead, maybe, but there's still one heck of a lot of money around which someone might pay for her safe return."

Joe looked at me keenly. "Then your little

friend Honey tells me you've been dancing and singing along to Ferdy Majik, and you remember his music, and Beatrice reckons your name is Lexi. This all starts to add up in my head, because I seem to remember that Ferdy's daughter is called Lexi, but when I talk to Beatrice, she remembers you as Lexina with a gran called Myrtle, who once used the Shelter, so I decide it's just a case of me getting it all wrong and jumping to conclusions, as it doesn't make sense. But I ain't one to let go of a good idea easily, so I decide to come along and meet Myrtle for myself. In case there's any funny business going on.

"And just before I come, I see the little bitty story I told you about, saying this kid's gone missing, without explaining why, and using the surname Jones, and I think, Why, that's it! They've got to find her, but they can't let out who she is, so they are just putting out her name and description as if she's one of a million runaways. I swear it is the Lexi I know, and I'm going to find out who this lady is who reckons she's her grandmother . . . pardon me, Myrtle."

"No, no." Myrtle smiled. "You were right to be suspicious. After all, no one knew of my connection."

"If only *I'd* been more suspicious," put in Sarah. "Or watched the news a bit more closely . . . but we've been so busy, what with the decorating and reopening . . ."

I was still reeling, trying to take all this in. Was Joe saying I was Ferdy Majik's *daughter*?

"Well—am I Majik or Jones or what?" I asked finally, exasperated, and caught Lexina's eye. "And Lexina, too?" Which didn't quite make sense, but that was understandable, given the circumstances.

"Oh, my dear," said Myrtle, patting my arm. "You're Jones, of course. Ferdy Majik wasn't his real name—who on earth has a name like that anyway? No, he was plain old Henry Ferdinand Jones when Maria and I first met him."

"Then—then he *was* my—our—father? *He* was the man you passed me to?" I gasped. Lexina grabbed my other arm and bit her lip, waiting, as I was, for the final piece of the jigsaw to slot into place.

"I was getting to telling you, when that awful man arrived and interrupted," said Myrtle. "I didn't want to rush it, because it was such a lot for you both to take in—and to hear the news that your father was dead, after you'd grown up with him, Lexi, on top of hearing about the death of your mother . . . But yes, both of you, Ferdy Majik was your father."

THIRTEEN
Going Home

So much to get to grips with. And slightly different things for Lexina and me. Lexina had grown up with Myrtle, not knowing about her rich and famous father. I had grown up with Ferdy, not knowing about Myrtle or Lexina. Neither of us had known much detail, it seemed, about our mother's death. Neither of us had known about each other.

And over the past few days I'd been the victim of a car crash, lost my memory, nearly been hit by another car, witnessed a shooting, found a grandmother and a twin sister I didn't know I had, and been the target of a kidnap attempt at gunpoint.

I'd also made some good friends, though Honey had disappeared, and Daniel still needed visiting in hospital. The strangest thing to come to terms with, at first, was the fact that the police hadn't gone, of course, but were waiting outside the front door of the Shelter to protect me from further kidnap attempts, and to get me back home as soon as possible.

Beatrice and Sarah were keen to get rid of them—they were putting off anyone entering the Shelter.

But I felt suddenly as though the world was being pulled away from beneath my feet—the world I knew. What was "home," after all? I couldn't remember it. And what about Lexina, and Myrtle, the only living family I had now? I'd just found them, and I wasn't about to let them go that easily. Once the plan to take me home was broken to me by one of the policemen and Beatrice, however kindly, I dug my toes in and let rip. I wasn't going without a fight—why couldn't I just go back to Myrtle and Lexina's home? What about Joe—and Daniel, and Beatrice and Sarah? And I wanted to find Honey again—she didn't even know about any of this.

"Hold on, hold on just a minute," said the kind policeman, who was dressed in normal clothes, not a uniform. "I'm sure we can sort something out."

Myrtle was hovering in the background, trying to hold back Lexina, but failing. She was clutching one of my hands as tight as she could.

"I think I am her next of kin, bar Mr. Jones's parents," she put in quietly but firmly.

"Mr. Jones?" asked the policeman, looking confused.

"Mr. Majik, if you like. I don't know if he has any living relatives. But at the moment, I am all she has. I have brought the girls' birth certificates, and my daughter's, and my own ID, which should prove everything I say." And she rustled in her bag and came out with an envelope.

Joe coughed and helpfully put in, "According to the star's life story, his mother died a few years ago—he wasn't in touch with her much, anyway—and his father died when he was very young, in jail, I believe."

"Right," said the policeman, and sighed. "Let's have a sit-down and a look at all this."

The upshot was the police didn't think it entirely safe just to hand me over and send me to live in Myrtle's two rented rooms in Old Town, considering what had just happened. They asked if she would be so good as to accompany me, with Lexina, back to my home north of Sweetside, which had "more adequate security," as they put it.

Myrtle nodded with no fuss at all.

"Of course. Besides, Lexi needs to go home. She needs to get her memory back. Is that all right, Lexi, Lexina?" she said, turning to each of us.

"Brilliant," we said together, and everyone laughed, just because we were twins and said the same thing at the same time. This was something else we'd have to get used to, I could tell!

After a lot of hugging and kissing, with the evening starting to crowd out the afternoon light, we set off in the car, all three of us in the backseat, and with police cars in front and behind, accompanying us as if we were famous or something. Lexina squeezed my arm and said, "Just think! Ferdy Majik's house! We get to see round it! Well, it's my first time, I know, and not yours. But still exciting for you, too, because now you might get your memory back."

"Yes," I said, fidgeting.

"Yes," said Myrtle understandingly. "And with that, of course, Lexina dear, it's likely it'll bring some sadness, too."

I don't know why I thought the journey would be longer—perhaps because the world I'd been in for the last few days had seemed a million miles away from anything I'd known—but it wasn't long at all before the small road we took off the huge, fast one started to look familiar, and then we were in front of a big pair of wrought-iron gates. I started to hop about in the backseat. I recognized the private track we'd driven in on, the big lanterns on the brick columns either side of the gates, the intercom the policeman had to talk into.

"I remember being in the big car," I said to anyone listening. "Dad used to just press a button for the gates to open."

And in my mind's eye, I saw the back of his head—Ferdy Majik as he was known, but Dad to me—and heard him saying, "Darn these gates. Seem to take longer every time," as he pressed a remote control.

And so the twinge of sadness began, and

increased as we drove in at last, up the long drive-way where I'd ridden my little bike when I was younger, past the tall shrubs and trees which hid the house—I'd made dens in their shadows, on the dry earth, which showed their roots from time to time like gnarled fingers.

There was so much to take in.

The house loomed up, huge, white-painted, with a sloping, green-tiled roof. The front door—like something you have on a church or castle, all arched and solidly wooden, with those massive black iron fittings—was standing open. It was like it was waiting for me to walk through, into another life. And it was scary. Above it hung another big lantern and security cameras.

I clunked the car door shut and that, too, seemed terribly important. The sound of closing off another life, an escape route.

But then, in the doorway, was the slight figure of a woman, young and pretty, with dark glossy tresses and big, doe eyes, full of worry. Now I saw her, I remembered her straightaway. It was Adelina, the housekeeper and my nanny, and I rushed into her arms, which, like Myrtle's, were skinny but crushed me so much I could hardly breathe to power my sobs.

Once that was all done with, and we were inside, Myrtle and Adelina ended up talking in the kitchen, so me and Lexina wandered from room to gracious room, dragging our fingers slowly along marble, or carved oak, over figurines and brass light fittings, me remembering, Lexina simply wondering at it all.

Here was the wide grand staircase, white and gold, like something in a film, where I'd been told off for sliding down the banister (fair enough, as there was quite a fall onto the black and white marble-tiled floor of the vast hall below).

Here was a TV room like no other—the screen took up a wall—and there were white leather sofas, sheepskin rugs and huge cushions scattered over a floor which had real cowskin—I mean, with the fur, brown and white patches and everything—covering it just like a carpet.

"Ugh!" said Lexina.

"Mmm," I agreed, looking at it as if I'd never

seen it before. Nice to stroke, but I wasn't sure about the smell. Also, I was possibly too fond of cows to feel comfortable about it.

I was gathering speed now, with my memory. I was starting to remember things before I saw them.

"I think," I said to Lexina, "somewhere through here—there's a proper cinema..." And there was—Ferdy Majik's own private cinema, with about six rows of red plush pull-down seats sloping down to the screen, which wasn't quite full-sized, and proper cinema lights and curtains which opened and closed over the screen when you pressed a button. Which we did, quite a few times.

"Dad showed his friends his own films here, before they'd go out on general release," I told her, remembering the chatter and the laughter, and the hush when the film started, and how the brilliant screen danced in people's eyes as the lights were dimmed. Ferdy Majik had starred in several films made by a company he'd set up himself—mostly comedies, for kids and family audiences, so I'd be allowed to watch them too.

We drifted on to the sauna and the gym and the

indoor pool; it was getting dark now, so I just pointed out of the windows of the huge glass room we'd called the sunroom, stuffed full of orchids and exotic plants, to show Lexina where the outdoor pool lay glittering darkly in the gardens beyond.

"Sometimes there would be parties," I remembered. "And he had the whole garden lit up. Real big torches burning, like you see in films. And peacocks wandering about between the guests. They made a heck of a noise. The peacocks, I mean, though so did the guests, come to think!"

We found my bedroom—huge and pink and white, with yet more marble, and more sheepskin throws and cushions over the bed and floor, and masses of stuffed toys piled neatly, including a giant dog and a smaller but very realistic tiger.

I showed Lexina my music player, which had hidden speakers built into the walls so the sound encircled you, and a cabinet which opened to show a big TV screen.

Then we sat on the bed and swung our legs and went a bit quiet.

"It's very nice," said Lexina eventually. "It's lovely, isn't it?"

"Yes," I said. "Though I'm remembering that it just used to seem normal. How strange. It's like looking at everything through two people's eyes; Lexi before the accident, and Lexi after."

Lexina looked at me again.

"You—you're not madly happy, are you?" she said gently. "Are you remembering your—I mean our—dad? Does it hurt to know he's gone?"

I looked down at my boots. I remembered now that they were designer, made to measure, and had been very expensive. Like the rest of my clothes. Dirty and scratched and scuffed as they were, no one had noticed. The kidnapper from Sweetside had taken me for a poor person when he'd first seen me, lost and needing help. He hadn't cared, because as a poor person, he thought I was worthless. He'd only come looking when he thought I was worth money.

"Lexi?" came Lexina's voice again.

"Sorry," I said, looking back at her. "I was just

thinking. No, I tell you what the problem is, Lexina. I do remember him. And I am sorry he's gone. But it's strange, it's like—like I have a distant feeling about him. I can't really explain. Like someone you knew long ago, but haven't seen for so long; by the time someone tells you they've died, it doesn't touch you that much. And then I feel a bit . . ." I trailed off.

"Guilty?" asked Lexina.

I nodded.

"I suppose so. Maybe it's the bang on the head, or something, but I can't seem to feel very sorry, to miss him very much."

"That is because you didn't see him very often, or know him that well," came a voice from the doorway.

We both jumped.

It was Adelina, with Myrtle behind her.

"I was just telling your grandmother here—Mr. Majik was always away, always working, always busy. He wasn't a—well, a natural father, a dad. He did his best by you, Lexi, but left it up to nannies and tutors to keep you occupied. He feared for your safety, and the dangers of growing up to be a celebrity because of who your father was, so he protected you from that. But in doing so, he cut you off from the real world. We argued about it many times." And here Adelina sniffed into what looked like a duster she was clutching in her hand.

"I don't say this to mean badly of him, you understand," she said in her strange English, dabbing at a blobby tear. "He did everything he thought was right and was the best for you. I just say it so you—understand your feelings toward him. He wasn't a stranger to you, but he was like—say, a kind uncle who visits occasionally."

"Oh!" I said, and felt a little better.

"He did many marvelous things—the music, of course, the record company, publishing and film and so on, much charity work. I will go through it all with you and Lexina, and so you will know everything about your father." She finished her serious little speech and gave us both a smile suddenly, and added, "One thing he got right, Lexi—you turned out a very nice girl, not spoilt and horrid like some rich people I have worked for.

And now there are two! Is it possible"—she looked to Myrtle—"that you will all come and live here now?"

Me and Lexina stared at our grandmother, stopped swinging our legs and held our breaths.

"It's possible," said Myrtle slowly. "Though I'm afraid you'll find Lexina here isn't like her sister at all. Spoilt rotten, she's been, a proper little princess!"

And then Adelina, looking shocked, saw me and Lexina starting to laugh, and Myrtle's mouth twitching at the corners, and she started to laugh with us, which is when I knew we were going to be a good team.

FOURTEEN
Beginning a New Life

The days which followed were busy and confusing.

"Who's that?" I whispered to Lexina as we stopped halfway down the stairs, watching yet another man in a dark suit being ushered through to one of the large rooms to see Myrtle.

Lexina shrugged.

"Search me," she said. "There seem to be loads of them, don't there? Let's ask Adelina."

"I tried when the last lot came," I said, "and she just said something about the Business, the Will and the Trustees—whatever they are."

"Sorting out the money," said Lexina, nodding wisely. "I mean, they'd have to, wouldn't they?"

Lexina was like that—sensible, and she put things clearly. I was so relieved when she and Myrtle had moved in properly.

She also knew what was worth worrying about and what wasn't, and set in motion her own little plans. Like now, for example.

She hitched one of her scrunchies more tightly in her hair and eyed me keenly.

"Come on," she said. "While they're busy."

"Come on where?" I asked, but as usual, she just scooted out the front door without answering, so I followed.

Around the side of the house she went, then suddenly across the lawns and into the shrubbery which bordered the high wall. I ducked under branches and battled with leaves in the face until I practically trod on her.

It was amazingly dark in among the plants, out of the bright sunshine of the day.

"What on earth are you . . . ?" I began, wiping a tiny insect from my eye.

"Shhh!" she commanded. "Give me a boost up!"

"What?"

"A boost up—so I can see over the wall."

"Oh—hang on a minute—I think there's a tub—over here," I said, remembering. It seemed a long time ago now, but I had played here. I pushed past a few more bushes and found the large plastic tub. We swept off some rotting leaves and dragged it toward the wall, with a few shrieks from Lexina when she accidentally put her hand on a slug which had been hiding under one of the rope handles.

"Shhh, you said," I reminded her sternly.

Lexina pushed the tub into position, upside down, and climbed on top. She could just about see over the wall. I clambered up next to her with difficulty, because there was only room, it seemed, for three feet—or one and a half people—on the upturned base of the tub. I wobbled.

"What are you looking at?" I whispered.

"Here they come," she hissed back. "Be quiet and don't let them see you."

I looked up and along the road. I could only see a few schoolkids straggling along.

I kept quiet, jiggling dangerously on one leg, until they had gone past.

"Well?" I asked. "What about them? Do you know them or something?"

"It's detective work. Preparation," Lexina started to explain, but at that moment the great detective lost her sidekick very suddenly. I'd put my

157

other foot down, forgetting there was nothing to tread on, and stepped straight into thin air.

"Are you all right?" she asked, looking down at me as I rolled about on the ground. She was giggling already.

"Yes, luckily," I said with as much dignity as I could manage, jumping to my feet. "Just a bit tired and having a quick lie-down. Now, why are you spying on the schoolkids?"

"I want to see what they are wearing," she said, hopping down from the tub and picking bits of leaf off me.

"Why?" I asked irritably. I seemed to have got most of the ground off myself, but kept getting that creepy-skin feeling as if an earwig or ant was under my clothes.

"Because Myrtle is up for sending us to school, I think, if we want to go. Well, I want to, at least. You—she's a bit worried you'll want a tutor again, as you're not used to school." She nibbled her bottom lip—I noticed it was a habit of hers when she was anxious or thoughtful.

"If you're going, I'm going," I said firmly, giving up on the search for the creepy-crawly.

You'll think I'm mad, maybe, if you're not a fan of school, but think about it. How would you feel if you found your cell phone, and the only contacts you had in it were your dad and the housekeeper? Anyway, I wanted to be with my twin from now on. We'd had enough time apart.

"Great!" said Lexina, giving me a hug. "I know it'll be scary for you—stop chewing your lip like that—but it'll still be scary for me, too, because it's a new school, and I'd rather you were there."

"I wasn't chewing my lip—was I? It's you who does that . . ."

"No, I don't," Lexina called back, trotting away again.

"Where are you going?" I called. "And yes, you do. Hang on, wait for me."

"Don't!"

"Do!"

"I'm going to tell Gran about the school idea. . . . And no, I don't-and-no-returns!" she called back over her shoulder, so obviously I tore off after her and we arrived in the hallway at about the same moment, and I had grabbed her by the shirt, and we were probably pretty loud, just as the Important Visitor was being shown out by Adelina. He was actually very nice about it, and assured Adelina he could dust himself off, thank you, but after he'd gone, she wasn't too happy with us.

"It's all right, Adelina," I said. "Lexina has a great plan. We will go to school and then we won't be under your feet so much."

"Oh!" said Adelina, surprised. She looked a bit worried, said "Oh!" a couple more times, then pushed us in to see Myrtle.

Adelina was all for it, though nervous for our safety. So too was Myrtle, it turned out. But between all of us, it was decided—no more hiding, no more deception, no more secrets. We'd go out there and face the world.

Then Lexina revealed the reason for her detective work—clothes. She'd already been to school, and she knew about fitting in. Our background would soon come out and people might be jealous or get the wrong idea. Having done her homework, Lexina announced her clothes were too shabby and cheap, and mine were far too expensive.

"Hmm," said Myrtle. "Well, while all the things to do with the will and money are being sorted out, I've been put in charge of an allowance—far more than necessary, in my opinion—for both of you. I'm sure we can sort something out."

"Great!" we said.

"But first—Lexi—I believe that someone is asking after you in hospital."

"Daniel!" I shrieked. "Is he all right? He asked for me?"

"Apparently, yes. I got a call from Sarah just now. Um—now, how to get there . . ."

"The driver is available," put in Adelina.

"The driver! The cars! Oh, dear me, yes," said Myrtle. "I'll never get used to it. Thank you, Adelina. Would you like to go with Lexi, if you wouldn't mind?"

"Of course not—I mean, yes, of course I wouldn't mind," answered Adelina with some confusion. Myrtle couldn't really get used to the idea of treating Adelina as "staff," and giving orders and so on. Adelina liked that, but was finding it strange. All of us were new at this. It was a bit like being put in a play all of a sudden and trying to play a role you weren't sure of.

Me and Lexina were forced to go and clean up a bit, and by the time that was done, the driver was waiting with the car.

His name was Tom, and he was new, so was only just catching up with all the developments.

"Who are you going to see at the hospital?" he asked, when we were all seated and buckled in to Adelina's satisfaction.

I explained.

"So this Daniel doesn't know about who you really are yet. And hasn't met the two of you together?"

"No, he didn't even know I had a twin last time I saw him. Neither did I," I answered.

"I never thought of that," said Lexina, and giggled. "It'll be a bit of a shock to him!"

We were still getting used to the impact we

could have on people as identical twins, and we hadn't even started on the pranks we could play.

As we pulled up in the hospital parking lot, Adelina said, "I hope the shock isn't bad for him. Maybe he will think he is seeing double, and still poorly!"

"What a great idea!" said Lexina mischievously. "You and Lexi could pretend you can't see me and don't know what he's talking about."

This brought on a swift pause and lecture from Adelina, adding that we were to remember what Daniel had been through, and weren't to tire him. So we put on serious faces and made our way along corridors and up in lifts until we found him in a side room, off a ward.

There he was, sitting up in bed, looking restless and perky, and not at all like someone who'd recently been shot. To our surprise—and perhaps my sister's disappointment—he took both of us in at a glance and didn't seem at all amazed by our story, just pretty pleased for both of us.

"But how are you, Daniel?" I asked. "Does it hurt?"

"No, it was sore for a bit, but not that bad. I'm just about fixed now," he said cheerfully. "But I think they might kill me with boredom." His bright eyes sparkled beneath the floppy fringe. Without thinking, Adelina put out her hand and pushed back his hair.

"This could do with a trim," she said.

And that one little gesture and comment was the start of it, for those two. I think she fell for him hook, line and sinker on that first meeting. They even looked alike.

Before we had left after that first visit, Adelina had tutted over his pajamas and promised a new pair when she next came, made sure he had chosen his meals for the next day, hunted out some paper and pens for him to do some drawings and was anxiously making inquiries about where Daniel would be going as he would soon be allowed to leave hospital.

She found out that Daniel was an orphan, or as good as. His mother had not yet been found, but the authorities feared the worst, and indeed she never was found.

164

To cut a long story short, Adelina talked to Myrtle, made a lot of phone calls, went off to see people and fill in forms, and Daniel was allowed, when he left hospital, to come back with us temporarily—after all, we had enough room—and after a while, Adelina was allowed to become his legal guardian, and he could stay properly and forever.

By the time Daniel came to live with us, our new school life was all flowing smoothly so that he fitted right into it like a little brother, though he had a tough ride at first as far as the schoolwork was concerned. I could cheer him up a bit, though, because homeschooling meant I was way ahead in some subjects and was behind—or had done something completely different—in others. With my, Lexina's and Adelina's help, he caught up all right and was soon winning prizes for art. He missed his real mother at first, but didn't miss lots of hugs and kisses, because Adelina was like that anyway, and ten times worse with Daniel.

Then there was Joe—it was all down to Joe that Lexina and I set out on the new pathway in our future lives. That sounds a great big deal, but it happened quite simply.

Joe came to visit, of course.

He arrived, acting rather shy, and after we'd all made a fuss of him, I realized why he looked different. He had gone to an effort with his clothes— whatever wasn't new was very clean, even if it was a bit faded and mended. He kept glancing around him all the time in an uneasy way. Of all the people who'd visited my proper home, Joe was the one who seemed to feel most uncomfortable surrounded by such a display of wealth.

After a while of having him being very polite, and hardly saying anything, I asked him if he'd like to come out for a walk in the gardens. This worked very well. We strolled down past the swimming pool and away from the statues and clipped shrubs and exotic trees to the wilder area which lay far below the house. Here, where there was a forgotten, damp old bench amid a tangle of wildflowers and grass, and surrounded by the chirrup of birds, Joe finally sat back and relaxed, letting out a big, deep sigh.

166

"Not really your sort of place, the house, is it?" I asked sympathetically.

"It's very nice," said Joe, being polite again. We watched as a robin flitted down close by.

"Is it?" I said. "I don't really know. I'm just used to it. I like this bit best. Maybe because it reminds me of the forest."

"Mmm," said Joe. "You never told me much about that part of your adventure."

"We never really had the time, did we?" I said. "For a chat or anything."

Joe gave one of his big, slow smiles.

"It was all a bit of a panic, as I remember." He paused as the robin hopped to the ground and looked at him with its head on one side; then he added unexpectedly: "I used to know the forest. My grandpa lived in a shack there when I was a boy."

"Oh!" I said. "Did you go there much?"

"Yes, all the time. Beautiful. Played there,—caught fish, watched the birds—" He narrowed his eyes as he talked, and I could tell he was back there, in his mind, a boy again.

"Birds?" I interrupted. "What sorts did you see?"

"Oh, all sorts—"

I interrupted eagerly. "Did you see one which was sparkling green and purple, with long yellow legs?"

Joe came back from his dreamy place and eyed me with surprise.

"A gallinule?"

"What?"

"You mean a gallinule. Purple gallinule. Walks on the lily pads? Yellow tip on a red beak?"

"That's it! It walks on the lily pads? OH! So *that's* how it does it . . . ," I said, laughing.

"And you thought it looked like it was walking on the water?" Joe grinned. "It *does* look like that, doesn't it? And in a way, it is, I suppose. I only saw one once. Now there's not supposed to be many left at all, in our forest."

I looked at him in surprise.

"Oh. What a shame! So pretty. So I guess I was lucky."

"I guess you were. There's another bird, called a lily-hopper, does the same trick, but not so pretty colored. I went back to my grandpa, and I said, 'I seen the prettiest lily-hopper ever.' And he listened and said, 'That's not a lily-hopper, that's a gallinule. Purple gallinule.' So that's how I know. Once seen, never forgotten."

We sat quietly for a while, thinking.

The robin grew bored with us and swept away to a bramble, where he paused to sing.

Huge white clouds like icebergs were floating across a brilliant blue sky. One cleared the sun, and a ray of warmth hit our heads so that we turned our faces up to it and closed our eyes, stretching luxuriously.

"Joe?" I said suddenly, without looking at him.

"Mmm?"

"Do you still visit the forest?"

"Not as often as I'd like. Things—work, chasing after stray children, stuff like that—seem to get in the way."

"If you did get time, and you were going, I'd like to come with you," I said, in a bit of a rush. I was just saying what came to me, without really understanding where it was coming from.

169

The bench creaked as Joe sat up.

"Hmm. Missing it, are you?"

I peered at him between my squinted-up eye-lids, trying to keep out the sun. I couldn't see more than a dark figure, but I guessed he was looking at me.

"Well—yes, I suppose I am. It feels like something's unfinished. In sorting out my head and memories. All that bit in the forest doesn't seem real, now, more like a dream. But it's true what you said about not forgetting," I said, still screwing up my eyes from the glare. "I've dreamt about that bird, Joe, when I was at the Shelter, and again since I've been here. And the funny thing is the forest seems more real in the dreams than it does when I'm awake."

"Mm," I heard Joe's voice say. "Might be good for you to go back, retrace your steps, have a bit of a think. I'll call you up and we'll do that. It'd be good for me, too."

I heard the bench creak again, and felt the wooden spars behind my back spread and bow, and knew that he'd leant back again in the sun. After a moment he said:

"You know, when I came across homeless people—and I've been near that stage myself a few times in my life—the way they live, it kind of reminded me of those sorts of birds. Lily-hoppers. They have big, wide feet with long toes to spread the weight and they don't stand too long on one pad. They keep moving, moving. They build a nest on a lily pad, sure, just for the babies—then they're off again. Can't stay still long or you sink."

"That's how it seemed for Honey's mum," I agreed, seeing what he meant. "I'd like to see Honey again, but it's hard to be friends if she's never going to be in one place. It'd be nice if she could end up like Daniel, settled, but there's not much I can do, with her mum the way she is." And I sighed.

Joe's voice came again, and I could somehow tell that he had opened his eyes and was looking at me, all from just the sound of it.

"Now, why do you say that?"

I swiveled round and squinted at him.

"What do you mean?"

"Why do you think you can't do anything to help?"

"I don't know. Her mum is a grown-up, I'm only just twelve. I can't tell her what to do," I answered a bit grumpily.

"But look at what you have here!" said Joe, his eyes wide, his hands gesturing to the space around us.

"Well, I suppose they could come and live here if they wanted . . . ," I said doubtfully, wondering what Myrtle and Adelina would think.

"No, no," said Joe. "I didn't mean that— the house and grounds and so on. I mean you have the businesses—the funds—the money—to make a difference. Not just for one or two people you meet—for all the people like them, that you haven't met."

At first, I thought he meant that we should give lots of money to homeless people to sort out their problems. But Joe went on to explain that it was much more complicated than that.

"There are lots of people who do have money, and aren't happy, or aren't wise with using what they have. 'Sides, what makes people happy, in my experience, is being able to look after themselves and their own family—not being given things. That don't make you proud, or feel you've achieved something. In fact, sometimes it makes things worse—makes you feel like a failure, because someone else has taken over and done everything for you. And money ain't all it's about. Honey's mum, f'r instance—like a lot of homeless people—has other problems to sort out first: fears, unhappiness and drinking too much."

I felt very young suddenly, and it all sounded too big, too complicated, and I thought someone else should deal with all these things.

Joe sighed and settled back on the bench again with his hands behind his head, and closed his eyes.

"Yes, well, I suppose you could leave it up to the Warrior Angels. And the Blue Lady."

I frowned. "I don't believe in that kids' stuff, Joe. You and I both know. The Angels didn't help

Daniel, and the Blue Lady was Myrtle. There's no such person as the Scarlet Prince, either—'Mr. Jones' was just a nasty, greedy rich man, who'd made his money from cheating other people, and was greedy and lazy enough to want to kidnap someone to get more."

"Well, I don't know about all that," yawned Joe. "Maybe the Angels did help Daniel—he got shot, but he didn't get killed. The stories do tell you to look out for big, dark cars with blacked-out windows, and that's true enough. They're always driving by and shooting people. And why can't the Blue Lady choose to be Myrtle, for once, in a way? She did save you. And Mr. Jones did a pretty good impression of that Scarlet Prince guy in the stories."

"What are you saying?" I peered at him, exasperated. "Are you trying to tell me a bunch of fairy stories are true?"

"True?" said Joe, without stirring or opening his eyes. "Well, got a lot right, didn't they? I like the warning about the old fridges being portals. Kid gets in one of those on some waste ground, to hide, and the door shuts, he ain't never gonna get out, suffocate just like that. It's happened. True ain't the point. It's just they put things in a way a kid can understand. So I ain't saying there are no Warrior Angels. I'm just saying, perhaps they need a bit of help every so often. Especially as Mr. Scarlet Prince seems to get a lot of help from ordinary people. But you say it's up to someone else. And that's the trouble," sighed Joe. "Everyone thinks it's someone else's problem. Then nothing gets done."

I thought for a moment, not happy to leave it on that note.

"Except, I suppose, the kind people Beatrice talked about," I said carefully.

"What kind people?" asked Joe without opening his eyes.

"The charity—the people who gave things—to run the Shelter."

"But it isn't enough," said Joe. "It's not much. Just the bottom part of a building. Just a place to stay a night or two."

"It was *something*, though. Better than nothing. It was enough for me," I answered.

Joe opened his eyes and looked at me sideways.

"Then why not keep it simple?" he said. "Start there. With just that building."

"That's an idea," I said, getting really interested now. "They said they never had enough space for everyone they could help. *I* said it was silly having the top of the building all empty when people were sleeping on the streets."

Joe turned around again to face me, looking interested.

"What would you do?" he asked.

"Well, get the rest of the place done up."

"Hmm," said Joe. "And you make it bigger, you'd need more staff, of course. Got to pay them, though you get nice people who will help out for free from time to time as well. Bigger kitchens. More food . . ."

"Beds and so on," I said. "More bathrooms."

"Of course," said Joe. "What happens if people like it and stay? They may never be able to afford rent outside the Shelter."

"Hmm," I said. "I suppose they could only stay

awhile. So other people get a turn. Just for the really needy . . ."

"So will the people leave your building, up and take the kids, and trot off to another one?" asked Joe. "Shame the kids don't get to go to school, and live in the same place as all their friends."

I thought for a bit.

"Sarah and Beatrice would know best," I decided at last. "Perhaps while the people stayed, they could get good jobs. Then they could afford their own place."

"Some of them can't get good jobs because they have problems. Or they didn't have an education," said Joe doubtfully. "Otherwise they wouldn't be in the situation they're in."

"Well," I said, "we'll have people to help them sort out their problems. And if they're not too old, couldn't they catch up with the stuff they missed, like school? Or wouldn't they like that, as they're grown up?" I hoped Joe wouldn't laugh at me.

But he was looking thoughtful, pinching his

bottom lip between his finger and thumb. Finally, he raised his big, brown eyes to mine and said, "No, I think they wouldn't mind. I think people run courses like that—training, they call it, computers, car engines, whatever you like."

Then he lost his serious face, and gave me the first old-Joe, brilliant-sunshine smile since I'd seen him back at the Shelter.

"I think you might have something here. What a brilliant idea, Lexi! Let's go and tell Myrtle—she'd have to talk about it with the people who handle all the money—and see what she says. I'll back you up, of course."

And so we did. It was only much later, when I thought back about this chat which would change all our lives—and that of so many other people I'd never met—that I realized how clever Joe had been, first making me think it was all my idea, and later, letting me take all the credit.

All I felt at the time was a rush of excitement at the wonderful plan, wanting to share it with Lexina, and Myrtle, and Adelina and Daniel, and most of all, if we were allowed to, Beatrice and Sarah—I couldn't wait to see their faces.

So I dragged tired old Joe, pulling on his broken boxer's paws, away from the wild garden, up the fine-mown lawns between the cypress trees and palms, to the house, with the robin's song lilting behind us and the sun shining down like it would never stop, to start the beginning of the rest of our lives.

FIFTEEN
Return to the Forest

The day that Joe rang and asked if I'd like to go back to the forest, autumn was truly drawing to a close. But today there was no rain, and still a little heat in the sun as it slowly burnt off the morning mists.

This was a special trip for me, and Lexina and Daniel were very grown-up about not coming, and solemnly waved to me and Joe as Tom drove away, on the understanding we would all go together next time.

Myrtle had contacted the kind policeman who'd dealt with everything that terrible night at the Shelter, and he'd brought round a map he'd drawn himself, showing the exact site of Ferdy's and my crash, and Tom was fairly confident he'd find it.

We chatted away until we headed along the road which led out directly toward the forest, wide and curved like a pirate's cutlass, slicing through the ancient trees and the quiet and secret lives lived among them.

Me and Joe stopped talking as Tom slowed the car, pulled over for a moment, glanced at the map and back to the road and said quietly, almost to himself, "Yes, I thought so. Just round this bend. He didn't make the turn—easy to do if you're going too fast."

He glanced in the mirror at me, almost apologetically, and added, "I'll just pull over a bit further on, where it's safe."

Me and Joe got out carefully—not many cars seemed to pass, but when they did, they sped by— and picked our way across to the opposite side of the road where Ferdy had swerved, and I had ended up hurled out into the trees.

I don't know what I expected. Perhaps no sign of what had happened. Perhaps a memory. Certainly not this: no memory of the crash, but no doubt where it had happened, for here were still the remains of flowers, brought by people and left in bunches, in little baskets, in cellophane, with bows and cards and ribbon. Some had been expensive and exotic, some just from people's gardens; all were withering and rotting now, the messages melting away. We stood and gazed, drowning in the musty scent of lilies and compost, gasoline and earth, all mingled together.

We spent a little time trying to read fragments of the notes: "Thank you Ferdy for the music," "... for so much pleasure," "miss you ..." I paused over one and called to Joe, "There's one here saying thank you for his *wife*—they met and danced together for the first time to one of Ferdy's tracks!"

Joe looked up and grunted.

"That ain't nothing. One here reckons they owe their kid being born to one of Ferdy's tunes!" And we looked at each other and managed a smile.

"It's a bit strange," I said. "Like they think they knew him, but they didn't." I mean, I was his daughter and lived with him, when he was around, and I didn't even know him, it seemed.

"Recognize anything?" called Joe, at the edge of the trees.

"Umm—not out here. I only remember waking

up in the forest, flat on my back." I picked my way across the fume-blackened grass toward him.

"Skid marks end there," said Joe matter-of-factly, pointing. "I'm guessing you would have flown—hmm—say, over in here, between the trees. Let's take a look."

I followed him.

There wasn't so much a pathway, more a natural space where trees weren't. We walked on along it for a little way, the trees closing in, the air becoming cooler and fresher. Very soon it seemed we were a million miles away from a road.

I stopped for a moment.

"Well, I can't have flown, as you put it, very far, surely."

"You didn't wake up by the road, did you?" asked Joe.

"No. I'm fairly sure not. I took a little look around and wondered which way to go. I would have gone to a road straightaway if I'd seen it."

"Then I think you didn't fall very far, got knocked out, woke up and wandered around, like you were sleepwalking—then you blacked out or came over sleepy and lay down, then you woke again in the bit you remember."

"But I don't remember walking about first."

"Like I told you, with a bang on the head, it's like walking in your sleep. And later you don't remember a thing. Fella I knew in a boxing match got knocked out, said he was fine; later on someone who knew him saw him wandering about three miles in the wrong direction from his home, stopped and talked to him, and the boxer was very cheerful, said he was fine, just on his way to the kitchen to get some milk."

"And you think I must have got up and walked a bit—well, it makes sense. Wish I could remember. I'd know where I went," I said, brushing leaves and branches out of my path.

"Oh, I think we'll find it all right. This is the only simple way from where you'd have fallen. Hopefully you couldn't have done much else but go this direction. Shout out if you see anything familiar."

What, like leaves, ferns, moss? I thought, glancing around me. We walked on in the cool, green silence for what seemed like quite a while. The only disturbance was the sound of our muffled footfalls on the soft dark earth, our shadows breaking the golden dapples of light which flickered across it, and the sighing sweep of a leaf across our clothes.

I was just thinking it was a bit doubtful that we'd find the bit of forest I'd ended up in, when a small brown bird fluttered up suddenly from the undergrowth to my left and made me jump.

"Tweety-pie!"

"What?" said Joe, stopping and looking back.

The bird had landed in among the branches to one side of him; as Joe spoke, it took off again, and passed behind him into a clearing.

"I think—I think this might be it. Ahead of you. Where I woke up."

Joe turned and looked, then motioned me forward.

"You go first. See what you think."

I walked on slowly, past him and into the clearing.

I looked around.

Space with no trees. No particular path. The smell of rotting logs. And then—the waterfall of sound from a little brown bird, the notes of his song falling over each other.

"Well?" asked Joe.

"Yes, I think this is it. Weird. It looks—well, less fuzzy, for one thing! I can't believe that's even the same bird . . ."

"The bird?"

"Singing. I—I'm afraid I called him Tweety-pie . . . ," I said, feeling a bit silly now I'd admitted it out loud.

Joe chuckled and squinted up to where the singing was coming from.

"Little warbler. He was here before? You sure it's the same place?"

"Pretty much," I said. "Though I know it's not likely the same bird really."

"Don't see why not," said Joe. "Probably his territory here. And you woke up here—and then what?"

"Umm," I said. "I sat up and I was sick. Ugh. Sorry. You probably didn't need to know that.

Then I felt better and didn't know what I was doing, but had a feeling I shouldn't be lying there. So I got up and . . ."

"Which way did you go?" asked Joe, twisting around and looking for a path.

"Followed the bird," I answered, feeling rather silly again. "Well, there wasn't any strong reason to go anywhere else, exactly."

"Hmm," said Joe. "Interesting idea. Oops, and there he goes. Shall we follow him again?"

Without waiting for an answer, he set off, and I followed.

The way was tussocky and more tree branches lashed at us. I started to get out of breath and a bit worried. Tom was back with the car, waiting, for one thing.

"Joe," I gasped eventually. "You do know the way back all right, don't you?"

"I'm particularly keeping a record of it," said Joe calmly, stopping and rubbing sweat from his forehead with a mighty hand.

"I'm not sure this is a great idea," I admitted, trying to catch my breath, leaning with my hands on my knees for a moment. "I'm not convinced I could *swear* to this bird being Tweety-pie in an ID parade of warblers, plus, even if he is, there's always the chance that *last* time he was going to get his groceries or something, and this time he's going to—I don't know—visit his gran."

Joe laughed, a great, rich sound from somewhere deep in his chest. I looked over at him and smiled back.

"You have a point there," he said, "though I am a great believer in fate. And I think he might be going to play at the swimming pool, rather than visit his gran. Listen."

And he cupped his hand to his ear.

I straightened up and listened for a moment— and could just about hear a trickle of water.

"What happened when you followed him before?" asked Joe. "Where did he take you?"

"We did go past water. I had a drink at a stream. I saw pools—and the gallinule. It was a long way, and I don't remember all of it. I think I might have been doing a bit of that sort of sleepwalking you talked about, because sometimes, especially on the road later, I seemed to sort of come to, and wonder how I'd got where I was. But Tweety-pie took me all the way to the edge of the forest and then I saw lights, and that was Sweetside."

"Well," said Joe. "We don't want to go that far, do we? This was just so you could see that where you'd been was—is—real. Let's go and see this water, have a drink, then get back to the car. We can come whenever we want and explore."

"Brilliant," I said. "And we'll bring supplies. And you can show me the parts you know best."

So we set off again, and now the trickling became louder, and the trees and plants thicker and darker; only a few paces further, Joe stopped and said "Oh!" quite softly.

"What—" I began, but Joe turned and held his finger to his lips, so I pushed my way alongside him as quietly as I could to get a view.

Completely encircled by trees, there was a large pool, bathed in deep blue shadow, reflecting here and there the flickering green of overhanging leaves. Earth and rock rose up behind it, smothered in ferns and creepers, splashed with little volcanoes of vivid scarlet and yellow of flowers and berries, erupting in the secret darkness.

But it was the waterfall which caught your gaze so you couldn't look away. Like a slender ribbon of silver silk, twisting as it fell, it caught all of the dying sun's pale rays and held them to itself, scattering just a few fragments to the pool's surface, and the sound of its falling was like music, little notes rolling over and over again, forever.

Both of us stared, entranced. And the more I looked at the cascading water, the more I thought I could see something, standing beneath, or behind the fall. I narrowed my eyes and stared and stared.

"Joe," I whispered. "Do you see something? In the fall?"

"Some*one*," he said, unmoving. "I see someone."

I stared harder.

"I can't quite make it out," I whispered.

"Don't try so hard," he whispered back. "Then she is clearer."

I looked away and looked back again, more casually.

And I saw her quite clearly. Long streaming hair, soft blue robes, a pale face behind pale water. For a moment I was transfixed, frozen to the spot. Then the trees began to rustle above our heads and around the pool, as if a wind was touching them. I looked up and there seemed to be lights; little spots of light, glimmers of gold and blue flickering among the swaying branches. All at once I felt as if we were being watched.

"What—what are—" I began.

Then Joe suddenly put out his hand and pushed me back a little, and at precisely that moment the surface of the pool nearest us split apart and a great, greenish-black creature flung itself at the bank. We both took a big step backward, Joe almost treading on me.

The creature stood half in and half out of the pool, rivulets of water like muddy pearls dripping from his body. And now his jaws hung loosely open and he turned his fierce eye upon us, there was no denying it was an alligator.

Joe still had his arm across the front of me, and now he gave me a little push. I took a step back, slowly, carefully, with my eyes on the alligator, and Joe stepped back too. The creature didn't move. Backward we went, a step at a time, until we felt safe enough to turn and hurry back the way we'd come.

We didn't stop until we were all the way back to the first clearing.

"An alligator!" I gasped, looking at Joe. "I didn't meet one of those before!"

Joe pulled a handkerchief out of his pocket and wiped his forehead and the back of his neck.

"Is the alligator the most interesting creature you saw there?" he asked.

"Most interesting? Most likely to munch bits out of me, at any rate!" I said.

But I knew what he meant.

"Did you see the same thing as me—under the waterfall?" I asked, still panting slightly.

"What did you see?" said Joe maddeningly.

"*Who*, you mean," I reminded him. "You said

you saw some*one*. I want you to say it first, so you don't laugh at me."

"I wouldn't laugh at you," said Joe, then looked at my face and added, "All right then, I thought I saw a lady in blue."

"I saw her too," I said. "But how can it be?"

"Have you seen her before?" asked Joe.

"No—well, yes, maybe. Below the bridge, in the river, crossing from Sweetside to the Old Town. Have you?"

"I thought I did, just once, when I was a child, long ago," said Joe. "I am glad I came with you today. I told you it would be good for me. Did you reach that pool before?"

"No, definitely not. Other pools, but not that one. And did you see the lights, like something was in the trees, moving around, watching?"

"Maybe Warrior Angels. Their part of the forest is supposed to be secret and protected by alligators. And there was certainly an alligator." He put his handkerchief away calmly. I dusted down my trousers.

"There most certainly was," I said. "As real as a very real alligator." I looked at him and he smiled, and I smiled back. There suddenly didn't seem to be the need to say any more. I turned to head back to the road.

"Come on," I said. "Tom will be worried."

EPILOGUE

Since the day I ran to Myrtle with Joe's great idea, the famous Lily-Hopper Project has grown and become the huge organization it is today—it's now just a part of the mighty Lily-Hopper Foundation, which does much more than provide a quick shelter for the homeless.

We began with the Shelter in the Old Town. Once that was completed—the whole building done up and providing space for three hundred people—we started to buy up other properties to turn into shelters. There are now five big Lily-Hopper Shelters, but we hope one day they won't be needed anymore.

While people stay there, the children get an on-site school. And there's school for grown-ups, too, with help and training for all sorts of jobs.

Then we got some building companies interested, and they've built several developments— mostly apartments—of affordable homes. These are for sale well below the silly prices of the city, only to people on low incomes. Instead of paying rent, you end up owning a part of the place you live in. This gives you a chance to either stay, or sell your part and move somewhere else with the money. They are really nice places to live, and because the people who live there own a part of them, they are proud and keep them nice.

And Honey?

Her mum now works as an administrator for the Foundation, and she and Honey live in a large, airy apartment, close enough so that we can all hang out together as much as we want. When Honey's mum hears about someone in a shelter who doesn't think they can change their life, she trots out from her office and gives them her life story and tells them, if she can do it, anyone can.

Ferdy Majik already had a small charity of his own, where he took musical instruments and equipment which people donated and got them out to poor kids. We took that on and made it bigger—now the kids can use their own recording studio and get help from experts who give their time for free. Some of them are already stars in the making.

Some of the people in the shelters retrained but felt nervous about getting new jobs and so on, after so long out of work. We heard about a project which was trying to save and restore the forest to what it had once been. They needed volunteers to work there—clearing, planting and so on. Before long we had a waiting list of shelter people who wanted to help. I think all that was one of Joe's ideas, though he has a way, as I've said, of putting them in your head and letting you think they're your own.

And Joe? Well, he runs his own special shelter or, rather, permanent home. It's called the Lily-Hopper Residential Home for Retired Pugilists—that's boxers to you and me—and he has also set up a fund for younger fighters who have been too badly injured to work again, to support them and their families. That really was his own idea, and we helped set it up, but since then he's raised enough funds to make the place run itself.

Beatrice took time out from the Old Town Shelter to help him get it all fitted out and so on, and the two of them made a good team, but bickered all the time. One day, me and Lexina were over there helping, and Joe was trying to plumb in a tap, and Beatrice was telling him he was turning the wrench the wrong way, and they both got to arguing again, when suddenly Joe stopped answering back, crawled out from under the sink, wiped his hands on a rag and stared at Beatrice.

We thought he was really angry. Even Beatrice shut up. Finally he said, "Strikes me if you and I are going to carry on like an old married couple, we should do it properly, Beatrice."

And Beatrice put her hand to her chest and said all quavery, not at all like her normal self, "Now, what on earth do you mean by that, Joe?"

And Joe said, "Why, I mean we should get married, of course."

And that was that. I mean, they did. Me and Lexina were a bit shocked. For one thing, as I said, they argued all the time—though in a quiet, familiar sort of way, I admit, not like they were really angry—and for another, we thought they were a bit too old to be bothered with all that romantic stuff, to be honest.

But you can never tell, can you? And we are glad they did, because now they are together, we have a sort of extra gran and granddad.

Sometimes I get to thinking about everything that's happened and it's the oddest thing, but a lot of people—and some forest creatures—have ended up happier, all because I bumped my head.

Gran—Myrtle, that is—says that often happens. A bad event, just as much as a good one, can bring about a big change in your life, and so you should always give things time to sort themselves out before you shout and wail and complain. Because changes can be scary, but they can be good.

Right now, I'm lying on my back among the ferns at the edge of a small pool in the forest. It's a hot day, and the ground is soft and cool. We've all worked very hard to save the forest, and to put it back to the way they liked it. And now I can see them—two beautiful birds, purple and green, yellow and red, bright and sparkling jewels, stepping across the water like it's the easiest thing in the world, planning on making a nest. I'm glad there are going to be more of them soon. I'm glad they've decided to stay.

L. S. Matthews writes full-time in England, where she lives with her husband and two children. She has written three other books for young readers: *The Outcasts*, *A Dog for Life*, and *Fish*, which was named a *Publishers Weekly* Best Book of the Year and was a Borders Original Voices book.